Tempting the Sheriff

Book 1
Sherwood Forest Shifters

Anna Lowe

Copyright © 2023 Anna Lowe

All rights reserved.

Editing by Lisa Hollett

Cover design by Kim Killion

Contents

Other books in this series

Sherwood Forest Shifters

Tempting the Sheriff (Book 1)

Tempting the Outlaw (Book 2)

Tempting the Maiden (Book 3)

www.annalowebooks.com

Free Books

Get your free e-books now!

Sign up for my newsletter at *annalowebooks.com* to get three free books!

- *Desert Wolf*: Friend or Foe (Book 1.1 in the Twin Moon Ranch series)

- *Off the Charts* (the prequel to the Serendipity Adventure series)

- *Perfection* (the prequel to the Blue Moon Saloon series)

Chapter One

ROBYNNE

Nottingham, England

October 1193

Sunlight filtered through the woods, giving the autumn leaves a golden glow. As I crept toward my prey, the soft forest floor muffled my footsteps, and I flared my nostrils, testing the air. In human form, my nose wasn't as keen as my fox's, but shifting wasn't a good option right now. The odds of bringing down my prey were higher with my bow and a carefully aimed arrow, so human form it would be.

For now, my inner fox muttered.

A bird whistled, and I paused at a movement. There it was — a buck, lifting his head and the twelve points of his magnificent antlers to check his surroundings. The beast was stunning — too stunning, maybe, because it would make the perfect wall decoration in some greedy lord's castle, to be admired during feasts attended by brave knights and fine ladies.

Technically, the buck ought to be safe here in the king's forest, but outlaws didn't always play by the rules.

I grinned. Especially outlaws like me.

Castles... warm halls... brave knights and fine ladies... my fox side reminisced.

I'd only ever witnessed such scenes from the outside, but still. My old life seemed a hundred miles — and years — away. And a good thing, too. I'd never really belonged to that world, and I never wanted to. And I definitely didn't have the makings of — or the desire to become — a fine lady.

I wasn't all too pleased at having to flee that life due to a "crime" that wasn't my own, though. If I ever got the chance to get my revenge on the true perpetrator. . .

I cut off the thought there. This was my life now, and freedom was worth the few hardships of living in Sherwood Forest. There was really only one part of that old life I missed, and he was lost to me forever.

My brave knight, my fox lamented. *Daniel.*

I pushed the grief away the only way I knew: by inhaling the musky scents of the forest. Here, I had hundreds of unspoiled, untouched acres to revel in, with no one imposing rules except Mother Nature.

The buck shuffled, reminding me of my mission. I reached past the long, single braid that held my coppery hair, pulled an arrow from my quiver, nocked it, and drew my bow in perfect silence. Narrowing my eyes, I held my breath, counting my own heartbeats.

Then I paused. What right did I have to take the life of something so beautiful, so free? So like what I wished to be.

My stomach growled, and my fox side whispered, *Imagine it's our betrothed.*

I scowled. If that scumbag were in my sights instead of a mighty buck, I would have buried four arrows in his body already. No one would ever force me to marry, especially not a jerk like him, and especially not when my heart belonged to Daniel.

I took another deep breath, waiting for the tiny pause between heartbeats, when the arrow would be most steady.

Ready. . . steady. . .

Go is next, my fox prompted. *Let the arrow fly already.*

I aimed a moment longer, then let the bow go slack. Not today. Not that buck. Not by me.

I puffed out my cheeks, glad my brother and the others weren't around. They wouldn't understand, and I couldn't afford to show what they would call weakness.

2

Suddenly, the buck swung its head around, staring into the distance. A split second later, my inner fox went on high alert too. When the buck raced off in panic an instant later, I ran too — toward the disturbance, not away, because something told me trouble was brewing.

My lean frame made me a fast runner, but when I skidded to a stop a quarter of a mile later, I knew I was too late.

Robert! I nearly yelled at the man standing beside a carriage. Instead, I shouted into his mind, using the mental link all closely related shifters shared. *What the hell are you doing?*

The thing was, I knew exactly what my younger brother was doing, and my heart sank. He and the fools who called themselves the Merry Men were at it again — holding up a carriage that dared enter Sherwood Forest.

At times like this, I asked myself why I'd joined their band of outlaws two months earlier. But being on the run had left me with no choice. Besides, they needed a leader, and that sure wasn't Robert. I'd had no choice but to take over and do my best to whip some sense into the men.

In many ways, we'd made progress — building a sturdy roof over our outdoor meeting area, insulating the modest huts we used as shelters, improving our water catchment system, and stockpiling supplies for winter. At heart, the Merry Men of Sherwood Forest were like energetic hounds — able to perform as long as someone pointed them in the right direction. But left to their own devices...

Robert! I hissed into my brother's mind.

Too late. Robert pulled the carriage door open. The rest of the men formed a circle, arrows aimed at the carriage, its driver, and the three accompanying guards on horseback.

Not that a scream came from the occupants of the carriage. More like a giggle.

I rolled my eyes. Clearly, Robert was working his magic again.

You, my dear daughter, have the wit and cunning of your mother — bless her soul in heaven, my father used to sigh. *Your brother, alas, inherited only her charm and handsome appearance.*

3

It was true. Robert was blessed with perfect teeth, fine manners, and a husky voice that made women's toes curl. That and a shock of unruly hair that give him that roguish look so many women loved. And as the son of a wolf shifter and a half-witch mother, he had a spellbinding charm that few humans could resist.

Yes, Robert had it all.

Or, nearly all. When it came to brains, well...

"Ladies, I regret to say we must lighten your burdens," he announced, turning on the charm. "But women with beauty like yours hath no need of trinkets to augment it." He slid the ring off one woman's finger in a sensual gesture.

Another giggle sounded, accompanied by the flutter of eyelashes and a coy press of a hand against an ample bosom.

I made a face. Seriously? They were falling for that?

They are, indeed, my fox sighed as the second woman handed over a pair of pearl earrings.

"Thank you, ladies. I can assure you your donations will be put to just cause," my brother gushed.

I snorted. To Robert and the others, *just cause* translated to drinking, eating, and making merry.

At his flirty urging, the women produced two sacks of coins, a silver comb, and even a ruby necklace. They only protested when it came to more personal items.

"That ring was my grandmother's," one explained. Apologetically, like *she* was the one doing the robbing.

"So sorry, m'lady." Robert held the ring to his heart as if he shared her loving memories. "But I'm sure she would have wanted good to come of it. Real treasure is the satisfaction we get from giving, don't you agree?"

The woman did — profusely, though her friend was a little slower to hand over the diamond-studded unicorn brooch Robert turned his eye to next.

"This brooch was given to me by my dear Richard, gone off to the Crusades."

Robert's jaw went slack, and I nearly buried my face in my hands. *Not King Richard, you idiot. It's only the third most common name in England.*

"Oh, not that Richard," the woman clarified. "Just my darling betrothed. Whatever will I tell him when he returns to find it missing?"

Robert flashed his most brilliant smile. "Are the Crusades not about fighting for a just cause?"

I snorted. From what I'd heard, the cause wasn't as just as some made it out to be.

"And will you not feel proud, playing your own small part in a similar crusade?" Robert laid it on thick.

The foolish girl decided, yes, she would, and handed it over.

I looked at the carriage driver, hoping he would mount a little resistance. But the old man wasn't interested in preserving anything but his own skin. And as for the trio of young guards on horseback... They were too terrified to do anything but stare at the tips of the twenty-plus arrows aimed their way. Even their horses pranced nervously, making the leaves underfoot crunch.

Enough already, I hissed into my brother's mind.

They're rich. It's not like they need it, Robert retorted.

True, but I have my principles, I shot back. *Don't you?*

He flashed a naughty grin. *Not since I came to Sherwood Forest.*

I could have beaten my head against the nearest oak. If our father could see us now...

Or mother, my fox added sadly.

Robert didn't remember her, but I did. Sometimes I wondered how he would have turned out if she had been around to guide him. Our father had done his best, but his child-rearing had been a little rough around the edges.

"At least tell us to whom we entrust our treasures, dear sir," the second woman cooed.

I huffed. Not even my half-witted brother was stupid enough to reveal his true name.

Robert grinned and gave an exaggerated bow. "Robert Hood, at your service."

My jaw dropped, but my fox just sighed.

Never underestimate Robert's stupidity.

John Little, one of the Merry Men, had coughed to Robert in warning, but all that accomplished was garbling what the women heard.

"Robin Hood?" They tweeted like a couple of birds.

I buried my face in my hands instead of yelling, *No, Robert. The idiot's name is Robert. I'm Robynne, and I want nothing to do with this.*

My God was I going to kill my brother.

From my left, hoofbeats thundered, and the Merry Men swung their bows in that direction. One of the carriage guards started to draw his sword, prompting the men to swing back again. Confusion ensued, so I stepped closer, barking for half to aim at the new threat and the other half at the carriage.

Good plan, John Little murmured — a huge, hulking bear shifter and the only member of the Merry Men with half an intellect.

Little John, the men called him. *If not the size of his body, then the size of his privates.*

Only a man that big and confident could take so much teasing in stride. On a certain level, we were all equals, but in the real pecking order, John was my second-in-command.

We were all shifters. All outlaws. All trying to forge a new life under the oaks of Sherwood Forest.

If only we all shared the same goals, such as keeping a low profile.

But by then, I had no choice but to draw my bow, keeping it steady as a single rider appeared at the curve in the road, galloping toward us.

And, wow. If ever our beloved, perpetually absent king needed a shining example of a brave knight, this man was it. His dark, flashing eyes practically yelled, *For King and Country!* and *Never surrender!* One tug of his thick arms brought his powerful steed to a halt, and for a moment, it seemed as if they both pawed the ground, eager for battle.

Pretty impressive, I had to admit, though I wouldn't be caught sighing dreamily like the two ladies in the carriage. My heart might have beat a little faster, and if I licked my lips... Well, it could get awfully dry in Sherwood Forest.

Then my eyes caught the steed's gray dapples and the man's worn leather boots. I swept my gaze up over his broad, chain-mail-covered torso. He wasn't wearing a helmet, so I got a good look at his face and hair, the latter two shades darker than his leather boots and just wavy enough to fantasize running my fingers through.

But then my pulse quickened, and fireworks exploded in my head.

Wait. No. It couldn't be...

I stared. The man stared back, and the sounds of those around us faded.

Daniel. My lips formed the name, though no sound emerged.

Robynne. The sparks in his eyes danced the way they used to whenever we were together.

Daniel. My childhood friend, a dragon shifter, turned lover. My beloved.

My mate, my fox yipped happily.

I was sure destiny had stolen him from me forever. Yet there he was, atop aptly named Charger, staring at me with his mouth cracked open.

Apparently, he hadn't been killed in the Crusades. Somehow, destiny had spared him and graced us with a reunion.

Then carriage driver called out, crushing the boundless joy of the moment.

"Sheriff! Thank goodness you're here! These bandits are robbing the ladies!"

My heart didn't just sink. It crashed deep beneath the floor of the forest. Sheriff? My Daniel, my lover — was the local sheriff? The cruel, ruthless monster reputed to have beaten Nottingham into submission?

I looked him over again, desperate that this was a mistake. Anyone but Daniel.

But Daniel it was, and my soul filled with a mournful howling.

Of course, people changed. Heck, I had changed in the five years we'd been apart. War could have a profound impact even on the best of souls. But still. Daniel, the sheriff?

I looked him over. He was the same, but different too. Bigger, stronger, more confident than ever. Truly a man now, I supposed, rather than trying to look like one.

Not trying any more, my fox breathed, because damn, did he make a picture.

Daniel's sword arm twitched, and I could sense a counter-attack coming. One that wouldn't unfold well. Daniel would swing his mighty sword, and the mounted guards would finally spring into action. Arrows would fly, chaos would ensue, and whichever of the Merry Men survived would take no prisoners. I could already hear the ladies scream and the carriage horses whinny in panic. Daniel would probably be killed, as well as my idiot brother.

The funny thing was, this was an echo of situations we'd experienced as children. Robert causing trouble. Daniel playing knight, rushing to the rescue. Me doing my best to salvage the situation.

The difference was, these were real swords and razor-sharp arrows, and no one was laughing.

I drew my bow, aimed, and let an arrow fly.

Thwippp! It sliced through the air, passing a whisker away from Daniel's left ear.

The guards froze, the women screamed, but the chaos I had foreseen was averted.

"He's trying to kill the sheriff!" one of the ladies cried.

Daniel's eyes — blue as the sea in the midst of a tempest — met mine.

Not a miss, I barked into his mind. *A warning, dear Sheriff.*

His eyes flashed in anger and something else. Sorrow? Regret? Heartache?

I must have been mistaken, because the sheriff I'd heard about showed none of those emotions.

Acting sheriff, Daniel corrected, shooting the words into my mind.

I scoffed. Acting? From what I'd heard, the suffering of the local population was all too real. Everyone knew the sheriff's reputation.

"A good thing the archer missed," the second lady huffed. "He nearly killed the sheriff!"

Not he. She, I burned to correct her. *I'm a she.*

Femininity wasn't high on my list, and my woodsman's clothes didn't exactly highlight my figure, but I'd be damned if they took me for that most foolish of creatures: a man.

On the other hand, concealing my identity wasn't a bad thing, so I kept my mouth shut.

Robert grinned. "My sis— I mean, that archer — never misses."

I know, Daniel's eyes lamented.

I glared, because that was probably part of his act. That wasn't the man I'd pined for for so many years. That was a stranger, possessed by the devil.

Wait. Is that Daniel? Robert's belated realization burst into my mind.

No, I barked.

And bless his stupid soul, Robert accepted that as truth. An instant later, he was back to his original line of thought.

"Never misses," he assured the ladies. "See?"

With that, he extended his arm away from his body, turning the woman's ring so the open circle faced me.

I shouldn't have gone for the bait, but seeing Daniel turned my brain to jelly. I drew another arrow, whisper-cursed, and let it fly.

Zing! Thwack! The woman stared at her jingling ring, now pinned to the side of the wagon by my arrow.

"My word. What a shot," she gasped.

With a grin, Robert pulled the arrow free and pocketed the ring.

"Enough," I declared, turning my big-sister glare on Robert. "Release them. Now."

When Robert opened his mouth to protest, I drew another arrow and shot into the tree over the carriage. A branch fell, whacking one of the horses and sending it into a panic.

"Whoa! Whoa there!" The driver pulled on the reins, but the four horses were already stampeding. The carriage bumped down the road, and the ladies screamed in a way that would have been profoundly satisfying to the mischievous child I'd once been.

But times were different, and all I could do was glare at Daniel.

The three guards took off after the carriage, making Robert and the Merry Men back up before they were trampled. Only Charger stood steady while Daniel hesitated.

Robynne. Please. I need to explain, I imagined him whispering.

But there was nothing to explain. I'd heard everything I needed to know about the sheriff of Nottingham.

"What are you waiting for?" I pointed to the careening carriage. "Better get back on the job, Sheriff." I made a mockery of the title, and all the men laughed.

Still, a knife turned in my gut. How could I speak to Daniel like that?

Daniel's face went frighteningly hard, even expressionless. Finally, he gave Charger free rein and turned away, galloping out of Sherwood Forest.

I watched him go, and my aching heart went with him.

Chapter Two

DANIEL

Galloping away from Robynne was the hardest thing I'd ever done. Even Charger's heart wasn't in it, and he took off at his slowest canter.

But that was the thing about duty, and Charger and I both knew it. Sometimes — lots of times — you did what you hated, because it simply had to be done.

Like accepting the job of acting sheriff of Nottingham. Like dealing with arrogant, spoiled lords to make sure enough trickled down for normal folks to make decent lives for themselves. Like leaving home — and Robynne — for the Crusades before that.

Well, I was back now, dammit.

I'd spent weeks searching for Robynne after returning to England, only to find one cold trail after another. Somehow, the rumor had gotten around that I'd been killed in battle, and Robynne had left Locksley for parts unknown. Some folks claimed she'd run off to the Crusades, like the old miller who'd smiled fondly and added, *She always was a bit of a wild child.*

Oh, I know. I know better than anyone, my inner dragon murmured.

Yet others had reported her dead, and that had nearly killed me. Still, I refused to stop searching. Not until Lord Oakley, whom I'd served under in the Crusades, ordered me to take this temporary job in Nottingham.

They're in need of a good man to put things straight, he'd said, sealing my fate.

Judging by the rumors about the previous sheriff, that was a hell of an understatement.

So here I was, on my way to finding out for myself, only to stumble across Robynne in Sherwood Forest.

Robynne with her long, long legs, toned from so many runs in the forest. Amber eyes laser-focused on an impossibly small target. Stunning, copper-tinted hair that was the hallmark of her shifter species. . .

I yearned for more time to take in every perfect detail, except one — the fact that her fool of a younger brother was with her.

Charger snorted dismissively, and I patted his neck. He was right. Robert had always been in and out of trouble. Robynne had the brains, the wit, the courage, and the cunning of a dozen men. So what the hell was she doing with the bandits of Sherwood Forest?

Charger snorted again, as if to echo the miller. *Well, she always was a bit of a wild child.*

I felt a flash of a smile, then frowned again. I'd finally found Robynne, but her glare had cut me to the bone, and I hadn't had a chance to explain.

I'm not that sheriff, I swear. Only acting sheriff. Please, Robynne. Listen to me.

But there'd been no time.

I'd never met my predecessor, but everything I'd heard spoke of pure evil. Happily, he'd choked on a fish bone and died — an end far milder than the ugly deaths he'd inflicted on many. That had been three weeks ago, though his demise was hushed up by authorities for fear of civil disorder. In several more twists of fate, I had come along and been named sheriff, at least until a permanent appointment was made.

A little ironic, really. Most folks back in my hometown would expect me to be the one *causing* civil disorder, not quelling it.

In any case, those were all issues I would deal with later. Right now, I had four stampeding horses, three useless guards, two screaming ladies, and a runaway carriage to escort into

Nottingham. Hardly the auspicious start I'd been hoping for in my new job.

Luckily, when we all came careening through the main gate of Nottingham — sending chickens flying, pigs snorting, and milkmaids scurrying — and finally skidded to a halt in the market square, the carriage guards wildly exaggerated the number of bandits. The ladies babbled about my bravery, and the driver claimed I'd dodged Robynne's arrow. So, as far as establishing a reputation went, it wasn't as bad as I'd feared.

The villagers listened with wide eyes, while Giles, captain of the city guard, smacked a fist into his palm dramatically.

"Something must be done about those bandits."

His tone implied, *Someone else has to do something, because I sure as hell am not leaving the safety of the city.*

I sighed. So that was what I had to work with.

One of the ladies fanned herself. "His name was Robin. Robin Hood."

Robert, I nearly corrected her. *The moron's name is Robert. Robynne is the clever one.*

"He nearly killed the sheriff." The other woman whisked a hand past her ear, mimicking the arrow.

Too bad he missed, most of the villagers' expressions said.

Lord almighty. How much of a prick had the last sheriff been?

A rhetorical question answered by the worn town stocks, where petty criminals could be bound by hands, head, and feet and displayed in public. It was the first, in-your-face structure anyone encountered upon entering the market square. Obviously, many a poor soul had spent days — maybe even weeks — locked up there for some offense, real or imagined.

I took a deep breath. Never mind that, and never mind telling folks that Robynne was a she, that she never missed — oh, and I loved her madly.

Instead, I led Charger to a trough and offered a wide-eyed kid a coin to watch over my reliable companion. Then I ordered Captain Giles to show me to the sheriff's office and living quarters.

He grinned. "*Your* office, *your* living quarters."

I scowled. If he was trying to butter me up, it wasn't working.

"But first, sir..." he said gravely.

A sergeant came up and handed Giles a scroll and the heavy collar that marked its bearer as sheriff. Giles unrolled the paper with a flourish and read loudly enough for all to hear, "By order of Lord Oakley, and in the name of God, and the King of England, and our good Prince John, et cetera, et cetera..." He motioned vaguely, skipping a section. "You, Daniel Cook, are named acting sheriff of Nottingham until such time as a permanent appointment can be made."

Second thoughts rushed through my mind as I stared at the collar. Then I kneeled slowly and bowed to accept it. Every soul in the square went quiet, but I was sure I could read their minds.

One tyrant sheriff gone, and the next takes his place. Some things never change.

I stood slowly, fingering the intricate chain. The links were fashioned in the shape of intertwined vines and branches — a whole forest of them.

My eyes drifted in the direction of Sherwood Forest, and I pursed my lips. Then I patted the chain, making a vow to myself. *I'll make things change around here. For the better.*

When I looked around, a hundred skeptical faces glared back at me, and I sighed.

"Right. My office." I gestured to Giles.

The sheriff's office consisted of a couple of rooms opposite the market square, a handy location for keeping an eye on things. I ran a finger across the desk, leaving a line in the dust. Had the previous sheriff only been dead a few weeks or far longer?

Giles must have read my expression, because he chimed in. "Sheriff Turner preferred running things from his private quarters."

That was our next stop, up the long, winding road through the middle of the city. Here and there, a dirty stream slurped along, then disappeared under street level. I strode past shops, past a baker's, over the small bridge traversing an inner moat, right up to the... castle?

I halted below the menacing points of the portcullis, but Giles motioned me onward.

"This way, Sheriff."

Acting Sheriff, I wanted to say, but I was too dumbfounded. A feeling that only multiplied when he led me through the castle's great hall and upstairs to a suite of opulent chambers.

"This can't be right," I protested. The place was fit for a king, and I was merely sheriff.

Acting sheriff, my dragon side muttered.

Captain Giles shrugged. "Oh, it's not the official sheriff's quarters. But given that the prince visits so rarely..."

You mean the king, not his rotten brother, I nearly said, though I let Giles finish his sentence.

"...the sheriff moved in here. No sense letting all this go unused." He winked.

I didn't wink back.

"Oh, here's Mrs. Fielding, the housekeeper, and the staff."

Mrs. Fielding was an older woman who wore her hair winched back as tight as a Saracen war machine — and had an expression to match. Definitely not a woman to mess with.

She offered the tiniest of curtsies. "Good day, sir."

"Good day, Mrs. Fielding."

Her staff were three beautiful young women who kept their eyes on the floor. I expected Mrs. Fielding to introduce them, but the captain did instead.

"Mary, Isabelle, and Claudette. They're here to meet your every need." Giles flashed a lecherous grin while the girls twisted their hands nervously.

I stuck my hands into my pockets before I throttled Giles. Here we were in the final years of the twelfth century, and for all our technological advancements, society was still so backward. No wonder Robynne was out in the forest. How many more centuries would it take to treat women as equals?

With that, my thoughts drifted to my lover, and I had to wonder. Had Robynne chosen the forest, or had she been cast out like an ordinary outlaw?

Nothing ordinary about my mate, my dragon declared.

I coughed away a growl and forced myself to focus.

"I see," I said, buying time. Then I stepped to the closest of the three young women. Mary. "Have you worked here long?"

Too long, her haunted eyes said, although she couldn't have been more than sixteen or seventeen.

When she spoke, her voice shook as much as her hands, and her eyes stayed glued to the floor. "Not very long, sir. My father is a baker, sir. The one by the east gate. I used to work there."

She would still be working there if she hadn't been cursed with such beauty, I wagered.

"And you?" I asked the second woman.

Isabelle looked just as terrified. "Not long, sir. I used to work with my mother. She's a weaver, sir."

I nodded grimly, then waved to the door. "Thank you, ladies, but I will not require your services. You are free to go."

Giles started to protest, but I cut him off.

"The only staff a sheriff needs are watchful men at the gates and loyal guards to keep the peace."

With that, I motioned. The two girls stared at each other for a stunned moment, then walked away. Once through the door, they ran, and for the next minute, the only sound was that of their fleeing footsteps.

But Claudette, the third housekeeper, stuck out her ample bosom and ran a hand over her hip, drawing attention to her curvy figure.

"I'd be happy to stay, sir, and serve you all on my own."

Her glistening lips left no doubt what kind of services that might include.

Feeling sick, I dismissed Claudette curtly. Then I barked at Giles to show me the real sheriff's quarters.

Those, at least, suited me perfectly — three modest rooms on the top floor of a building near the city walls. It had two balconies — one overlooking the heart of the town, and a smaller one overlooking the walls — and beyond them, fields, the river, and Sherwood Forest in the distance.

Robynne, my inner dragon whispered.

The rooftops formed a continuous, crooked landscape, all the way over to the shadow of the church near the city walls — a place well suited to dragon takeoffs and landings.

"This will do perfectly," I murmured, to Giles's astonishment.

I spent the next hour tending to my highest priorities — finding the best stable for Charger and firing everyone except the worst of the domestic staff. Yes, the worst. That left me with Fitzgibbon, a half-blind, half-drunk fellow who wouldn't keep close tabs on where the new sheriff went or how or when or why.

Once all that was settled, I stepped onto the smaller balcony and gazed toward the forest. My senses went deaf to city impressions — the clatter of hooves over cobblestones, the stench of the gutters — while my eyes drank in the forest. The kaleidoscope of greens, the endless, undulating canopy. And somewhere beneath that, the camp of a band of outlaws.

Then I shifted my gaze to study the city walls. Did they function to keep free men in or out? Sometimes, I had to wonder.

But most of all, my thoughts were preoccupied by Robynne. By love and promises. By destiny.

Something must be done about those bandits, Giles's words echoed in my mind.

I nodded slowly, thinking of my long-lost lover.

My dragon rumbled impatiently. *Something, indeed.*

Chapter Three

ROBYNNE

I walked along the road to Nottingham, doing my best to stride naturally. Not so easy, given the way my pockets drooped with coins and other small treasures. But on I strode, a woman on a mission.

It had taken three days, but I'd managed to harangue my brother and the others into surrendering the loot they'd stolen from the women in the carriage.

But they're rich! Robert had tried convincing me. *They don't need more than they already have.*

Yes, John Little had agreed. *It's no sin to steal from the rich.*

It is, I'd countered, *unless you give to the poor.*

I'd spent hours working out a way to balance out our dark deed, if not actually undo it. After all, I might be an outlaw, but I was no criminal.

John Little had snorted at that. *What's the difference?*

In my mind, it was simple. *Outlaw* was a label imposed by a not-always-honest authority. *Criminals* were those who had truly sinned, whether they'd been caught at it or not.

At that, all the men had grumbled in agreement. *Criminals are the lords who rule this country, while honest commoners can barely earn a living.*

And just like that, the Merry Men and I had a new mission. But redistributing stolen wealth was easier said than done, as I realized upon approaching the guards at the city gates.

"You don't have to go through with this, you know," John muttered from over my shoulder. High, high over my shoulder. The man was that big, and even my long legs worked hard to keep up with him.

"Oh yes, I do."

I strode onward, leaning into the autumn wind and repositioning the sack slung over my back. It was full of finely spun wool — my ticket to Nottingham's weekly market. I could have arrived as an empty-handed buyer, but a load of goods would make the guards less apt to scrutinize me.

"Make yourself look smaller," I hissed as we approached the north gate.

John stooped, trying to hide behind the sacks he carried, cursing the whole time. He hated town. He hated humans. But he was loyal as hell and a huge asset in a fight — literally. Of course, his size also made him stand out, as did the scars on his mangled hand. Still, it was a risk I was ready to take.

We'd left camp at the crack of dawn and stopped at a tiny croft soon after — one so far from the city as to have virtually no protection from thieves and bandits.

Okay, okay. Technically, we were thieves and bandits, but we had our principles.

Bess, the young woman there — barely older than me, but already a widow with three young children — looked exhausted, and that was before carting her wool to market. Her eyes had gone wide when we'd promised to deliver it for her, leaving ten coins as our deposit and only one demand: no questions asked.

She'd clutched the coins to her chest and hurried back into her house. No questions asked.

I was sure the guards could hear my heart thumping as I passed, but no. As mere humans, they didn't have particularly keen senses.

My fox sniffed haughtily. *Not like me.*

Still, I kept my guard up.

The market square was a flurry of activity as vendors set up their stalls. It didn't take long to find the weaver Bess described and deliver the wool — again, no questions asked in return for a penny. Then John took up a watchful position at the head of an alley while I ambled around the marketplace on my true mission. Casually, I pulled a few coins from my pockets and sprinkled them through the rushes underfoot. Later, when the market closed, the poorest of the poor would sweep the area and find their reward. The same went for the vendors whose goods I pretended to study. Stacks of whittled spoons, bolts of cloth, piles of fruits and vegetables — all made perfect hiding places for coins dropped in for the vendors to find later.

But, boy. Redistributing wealth took forever. All the while, pigs squealed and chickens strutted underfoot. One cock kept crowing at me as if to sound the alarm, but no one appeared to take notice. Still, I was keen to get moving. The longer I wandered around the square, the greater the chances of being discovered. As a last resort, I dipped my hands in the fountain at one end of the square, letting the remaining coins gently sink to the bottom.

I withdrew my hands and shook away drops of water. There. Almost done. Just one more task and my work would be complete.

I ambled to the stocks, stopped, and stretched, discreetly looping two small items over a crosspiece of the contraption — the part where the criminal's left arm would be shackled. Then I retreated to a shadowy corner to watch and wait.

Wait, I did, for a good quarter hour. Anytime anyone lifted a crate or strolled by the fountain, I burned to shout or shake them. *Stop! Look! There!*

Either I'd hidden the coins too well, or the town was full of morons.

Finally, a young boy scooped a little water from the fountain, then kneeled and offered it to his dog. When he reached into the fountain for more, I leaned forward, praying.

Come on, come on...

The boy's bleary gaze suddenly went hawk-sharp, and his whole body froze. Then he reached deeper — almost shoulder-deep — and fished out a coin. He clutched it in both hands, staring.

Attaboy! I nearly cheered.

The sheer, innocent joy that dawned on his face made me glow in satisfaction. I glanced over at John, who was grinning broadly. When he met my gaze, he flicked his fingers to his brow in a salute.

Makes it all worthwhile, doesn't it? I whispered into his mind.

He nodded solemnly. *I get it. Now I get it.*

I pictured the villagers an hour from now, quietly patting little treasures they'd slipped into their pockets.

I motioned John toward the gate. *Go ahead. I'll follow in a minute.*

When the bear shifter lumbered through the gate and out of sight, I exhaled. Soon, I would follow, and we could bring good tidings to our friends in Sherwood Forest.

But a shout broke out, and then another, and the stir of the market turned into an all-out commotion. I edged forward. What was going on?

"Thief! Thief! Now we've got you!"

One of the city guards yanked the boy's arm so high, the poor urchin nearly dangled in midair.

Three more guards ran up, and everyone else shrank back.

The boy's body and voice trembled. "I didn't steal it, sir. I found it."

"Liar!" the guard roared, shaking him.

My heart sank. No, no, no! This was not what I'd intended.

The boy looked around desperately, but no one stepped forward. Everyone stared, frozen in fear.

I nearly burst out shouting. *He's an innocent child!*

Before I could, someone else strode forward.

"What's going on here?"

The voice was so powerful, so commanding, that most of the crowd dropped to one knee in a sign of deference, and the square went frighteningly silent.

I tensed, recognizing him. Daniel. Or rather, the sheriff. A different man from the one I'd once loved. The fear in everyone's eyes proved he'd become a cruel, heartless tyrant.

I gulped, fingering the bow hidden under my cloak. For years, I'd dreamed of a joyous reunion. Now, I wondered if I had what it took to kill Daniel.

One look at the trembling boy sealed my decision. Yes. Yes, I would.

"Now then," Daniel boomed, making the guards flinch. "What's going on?"

The guard shook the boy. "He stole that coin."

"I didn't!" he squeaked. "I found it. In the fountain. Look. There are others."

A pig snorted, echoing the guard's expression. Cruel, heartless men didn't bother checking for evidence.

But this one did apparently. Daniel leaned over and plucked another coin out of the fountain.

"Indeed," he murmured.

Every soul in the square held their breath, awaiting Daniel's judgment, as if Moses, Peter, or an even more powerful, all-knowing being stood there instead of a mere mortal.

My inner fox sighed a little dreamily. *Not quite a mere mortal.*

"I swear, I didn't steal. I found it, sir," the boy insisted.

I held my breath as I waited for the sheriff's verdict.

Maybe he hasn't changed. Maybe he isn't a tyrant, my fox whispered.

"Indeed, you did," Daniel finally said.

One hard look made the guard release the boy, who rubbed his shoulder. Daniel patted him on the back, then looked around, searching for the true culprit.

Time seemed to stretch, with every second cut and drawn into long, boundless subsections. Chickens squawked. A dove fluttered overhead, cooing. A crisp fall breeze tiptoed through the market, carrying the scents of spices, flowers, and garbage. Daniel turned slowly, taking in every detail.

His dragon eyes glittered, counting every hidden treasure at the bottom of the fountain. Then they turned, sweeping across the square until they came to rest on the items I'd left on the stocks. His gaze narrowed, and a moment later, something like wonder shone in his eyes.

Yes, I wished I could say. *That's the ring that lady's grandmother gave her, and the unicorn brooch belongs to the other, given to her by her dear Richard.*

Not the king, my fox threw in, as if Daniel were as stupid as my brother. *Her darling betrothed, a different Richard.*

No one had noticed those two little pieces until then, but my fox chuckled. *Leave it to a dragon to find the treasure.*

At that exact moment, Daniel shifted his gaze, landing directly on me.

I swallowed, staying perfectly still.

I hadn't moved or made a sound, yet he'd homed right in on me. Like the old days, when each of us knew exactly where the other was, because that's the way it worked with destined mates.

My breath caught. My muscles stiffened. My heart stopped beating. A moment of truth, and I knew it.

Was that the sheriff appraising his next victim? Or was it the Daniel I once knew — my Daniel?

A voice whispered through my mind. *Leave it to a dragon to find true treasure.*

Not Daniel's voice. It was deeper, slower. A voice from the bottom of the earth, like destiny.

You're my only treasure. Daniel's words, uttered years ago, echoed through my mind.

My cheeks heated, and my mind blurred. Then someone coughed, and I blinked as time took off again, moving at its normal pace, yet feeling like a hurricane.

Daniel tore his eyes from me and patted the boy on the shoulder.

"What you found fairly, you shall keep," he announced, loud enough for everyone to hear. Then he scanned the crowd with a dark expression that said, *Woe be the man who finds anything by any other means.*

When he pressed the second coin into the boy's hand, a murmur went through the crowd, and the guards looked flabbergasted.

"All right, everyone. Back to business," Daniel said a little more softly — though the look he shot at the guards was anything but.

He might as well have cracked a whip over their heads. *You will let these people go about their business. You're here to protect, not victimize.*

And just like that, the single point of everyone's attention splintered into dozens of separate fragments, and everyone backed away. Some returned to work, while others formed whispering, awestruck clusters.

Daniel let a few beats pass before glancing at me. A heartbeat later, he was moving in my direction.

I took off at a race-walk, trying to lose myself in the maze of the medieval city.

But some things you couldn't hide, no matter how you tried. Especially not when it came to destiny.

Chapter Four

ROBYNNE

I hurried down the alley and around the corner, desperate to avoid my ex-lover. But a few streets later, I slowed, took a few deep breaths, and stopped.

Cowards run from their enemies, my father used to say. *The brave face them.*

I gathered my wits and chose my ground — the first step up a covered staircase in a backstreet. As footsteps over cobblestones signaled his approach, I crossed my arms and raised my chin.

"Robynne," Daniel murmured, his voice not quite steady.

Good, because neither was mine. Still, I raised an eyebrow, trying to stay cool.

"Daniel." I let a heartbeat go by, then pointed at the heavy chain of office around his shoulders. "Or should I say, Sheriff?"

His expression went hard. "Acting sheriff."

If his word were text in an illuminated manuscript, *acting* would be big, bold, and surrounded by a dozen intricate figures.

He'd said it before, but it didn't really register. Now, it finally hit me.

"Acting sheriff... since when?"

"Since this week."

My gut flipped, and my cheeks burned.

"Oh." I sounded as lame as I felt. Still, I stood firm, glad for the step that put me on eye level with Daniel. Dragons might be high and mighty, but foxes were quick and clever. Proud, too.

Maybe too proud sometimes.

He leaned closer, making my heart race.

"You know what they say," Daniel murmured. "Don't believe everything you hear about the sheriff."

I had to give him that, but I couldn't resist a little challenge. "Don't believe everything you hear about outlaws."

He chuckled, but there was no humor in it. "If there's one thing I learned in the Crusades, it's not to believe what you've been told. About the enemy. About our own righteousness. About the way things should be."

I wanted to ask about those years he'd been away, but I didn't have the nerve. What had he endured? Who had he met? What had he done?

I was thinking along the lines of battles, but my fox wondered about women, and my heart sank at the possibilities.

"Right. Outlaws — including you." Daniel continued, looking so sorrowful, I was almost ashamed. "How, Robynne? Why?"

How did I end up a fugitive from the law, living in a forest with a bunch of common thieves? I often asked myself the same question.

I shrugged. "Long story." One I wasn't about to share. Which gutted me, because there'd been a time when we'd shared everything.

Then I stuck up my chin, because I wore defiance better than regret. "I can assure you, my only crime was standing up for myself."

Daniel raised an eyebrow. "And yet, you roam the forest. You steal—"

I cut him off. "Robert stole. I gave it back."

Again, the eyebrow. A tiny gesture that would have a dozen women swooning, though I was immune — or at least, good at pretending.

"Gave back, how?" he pressed on. "From what I remember, the coins weren't stolen from a fountain."

"You know what I mean."

He leaned a little closer, and his voice went all gravelly. "Why don't you explain, then?"

I stuck a finger at his chest — big mistake, because the contact sent little zings through my body.

God, was I in trouble. And not just with the law.

"Robert steals from the rich. I give to the poor. Call it a form of reverse taxation."

His lips quirked. "Reverse taxation. Authorized by...?"

I pressed harder with my finger, knowing those slabs of muscle would protect him. The question was, how to protect myself — especially my heart?

"Authorized by truth. By justice," I declared, hoping it was convincing.

He tilted his head, mulling that over.

I did my best to stay focused, but it was hard, what with his face within kissing distance. Some of the contours were familiar, like the jawline I used to run my lips along. Others were new, like the thin scar hiding in the stubble of his chin. Yet others were a mix, like his thick, dark hair, cut a little shorter than it used to be, but still the perfect length to run my fingers through.

I shook myself and cleared my throat. "I returned the only things those noblewomen would actually miss."

Daniel grinned. "That was a nice touch."

My inner fox swished its tail, terribly pleased with itself. *My idea.*

Actually, it had been *my* idea, but never mind. I went on making my point. "Money means nothing to the rich."

"It does when pride is involved," Daniel pointed out.

True. That was the tricky part of the bandit business, as I was starting to see. Hurt pride inspired vengeance, and sooner or later, vengeance would incite someone to come after the bandits of Sherwood Forest. But try explaining that to my brother and the other men.

Come on, Robynne, one of them had complained. *Robbery is our best form of entertainment.*

Our only *form of entertainment,* another had lamented.

I really, really had to come up with something more constructive for them to do.

Daniel shook his head sadly. "I'm all for truth and justice. But different people have different definitions of those things."

"What about you, Sheriff? How do you define them?"

He opened his mouth, then stopped and flashed a sentimental smile.

"No use arguing. You outfox me every time." Then his smile faltered, and he touched my arm. "Still, you must be careful. You'll get hurt playing with fire."

Fire? Flames were already flickering through my body, right down to my girl parts.

"Maybe I'm not playing. Maybe I just can't ignore what's unfair."

"Neither can I," he insisted. "But we must tread carefully."

My turn to arch an eyebrow. "We?" Slowly, it dawned on me. "Are you saying I'm not the only one with a mission?"

My soul sang, racing away with a thousand images of my true love and me righting wrongs, protecting the innocent, and otherwise engaging in noble pursuits.

Engaging in more than just that, my fox hummed, conjuring up images of our intertwined bodies.

That was the problem with being a shifter. The animal side had a one-track mind.

"I'm saying, I want what you want," Daniel said. "A better life for lesser-off souls. A clear conscience that I've done the best I can do." His blue eyes dulled, and his voice grew ragged. "But the Crusades taught me to beware of lofty goals and that things are not as simple as they seem."

I pursed my lips, knowing he was right. But what would I be without my hopes and dreams? *Who* would I be? Just another bystander, or the person I aspired to be?

I caught Daniel studying me, smiling. Then he cupped my cheek and stroked it with his thumb, whispering, "There she is."

Instinct made me reach for his wrist, ready to swat him away. But the moment we made contact, all I could manage was a soft caress.

Drat my body for betraying me.

"There's who?" I whispered.

His smile went all wistful. "The woman I fell in love with." His throat bobbed, and he leaned closer. "The woman I never stopped loving."

All the loneliness and sorrow of the past five years wrapped around my chest and squeezed. My arm muscles twitched, aching to hug my true love.

I missed you so much, he would whisper, his lips brushing my ear.

I missed you more, I would reply, though the end would be muffled by a kiss. A long, soft, hopeful kiss that tried to make up for five long, hard years.

But my words never made it past the lump in my throat, and the hug — and kiss — remained prisoners of my dreams. Because a scuffing sound signaled a passerby, and we drew apart, listening. The footsteps faded down an adjoining street, but I still hung my head.

We couldn't be found here. Not now. Not here. Not together.

Not ever?

My chest ached, and my throat bobbed.

Besides, I had to be careful. As strong as the pull to Daniel was, I couldn't allow myself to trust anyone — not even him. *Especially* not him, because a man as treacherous as the sheriff I'd heard about could try all kinds of tricks.

Gazing into Daniel's deep, solemn eyes, I found that hard to believe, but I had to consider the possibility. So I let out a long, steadying breath and forced myself to step away.

"I have to go. Someone might come." I glanced down the street, then up the stairway we'd hidden in.

Daniel chuckled. "The only person who lives up there is me."

My mouth cracked open. Destiny had guided me right to his doorstep. If that wasn't a sign, what was?

"So, now what?" I asked myself as much as him. "I'm a bandit. You're the sheriff."

"Acting sheriff." Then he forced a thin smile. "Remember about not believing what they tell you."

I nodded slowly. "You remember too."

31

Daniel might be back, and my heart would always burn for him. But I had grown — and changed — enough to know how to protect myself. Life wasn't a fairy tale. It was harsh. Relentless. Cruel, even.

But life was also what you made of it, as my father used to say, so I decided to start there.

"I won't believe what anyone tells me. I'll let you prove yourself."

Daniel nodded, accepting the challenge. "The same with you."

I nodded, stepping backward. I had come to town on one mission, but now, I had a new one. Proving my good intentions to Daniel — and making sure he proved his to me.

I shot him a wily grin. "Watch what you wish for, Sheriff. There might be more robberies along the Great Northern Road."

A crooked smile was his reply. "I don't know whether to hope so or hope not." Then he turned serious. "Either way, watch yourself, Robynne."

Images of marching soldiers, stomping steeds, and armed reinforcements flashed through my mind. Yes, I had to be careful. Very careful. But not just me.

"You watch out, too. There are traitors everywhere, you know." I pointed around, then at him.

Nodding wearily, he steered my finger away, as if he'd learned about traitors the hard way too.

"I will." His expression went sad, and his eyes roved my face for some sign of. . . love? Weakness? Regret?

When his eyes stopped, focusing on my lips, my heart skipped a beat. His throat bobbed, and mine did too. My body heated, and I nearly leaned forward, sure he would dip in for a kiss. A kiss I was desperate for — er, desperate to fend off, I mean.

The moment I caught myself, Daniel hardened his jaw and stepped back. "Until we meet again, Robynne Hood."

I dipped into my best curtsy, which wasn't very good. "Goodbye, Sheriff."

His lips quirked. "Goodbye, bandit."

I flashed a little smile then steeled myself to leave. One step after another, resisting the urge to peek back at him.

Not goodbye, his dragon whispered into my mind. *Make it until we meet again.*

I couldn't resist a little grin. Was that a challenge or a promise?

Either way, I nodded as I strode away. *Until we meet again, Sheriff.*

Chapter Five

DANIEL

Any average person's footsteps would have click-click-clicked over the cobblestones. Robynne barely made a patter.

Fox shifter, my dragon hummed fondly.

Her reddish-brown hair glinted, making me smile. But when she disappeared around a corner, I sank against the wall.

Robynne — my Robynne — was back in my life. I closed my eyes, savoring the fresh memory of her scent, her soft touch, her voice — a little grittier, a little sadder, but as firm and commanding as ever. I'd nearly kissed her, and although the timing had been bad, I regretted missing my chance now.

It was the perfect time, my dragon insisted bitterly.

Not exactly, but dragons tended to act first and think later.

Says the fool who gallivanted off to the Crusades, the beast sniffed.

I made a face. Touché. But it had seemed like the right thing at the time. How else was a man like me — no land, no title, no money — to make something of himself?

My eyes slid shut as the few highlights — and many low points — of those five long years paraded through my mind. Lots of *hurry up and wait,* lots of pining for home, interspersed with brief moments of sheer terror, elation, or raw adrenaline.

Five years of yearning for my mate, my dragon lamented.

Well, I was back now, and I was going to make the most of it. Somehow.

I glanced up the stairs, tempted to sprint up to my north-facing balcony for a last glimpse of Robynne. But that meant more waiting, watching, and hoping. I'd done too much of that in the past few years, and what had that accomplished? Now, I was my own master, and every action I chose laid another stone in the path to the future I desired.

Which was... what exactly?

Robynne, my dragon growled, focusing on the *desire* part.

My body heartily agreed, a grim reminder of five lonely years without my mate. Otherwise, the details were blurry.

The details don't matter, my dragon insisted.

I nearly laughed out loud. With Robynne an outlaw and me the town sheriff... I rubbed my temples. Boy, did those details matter.

The first action I decided on was returning to the market square to observe ordinary citizens, and, even more importantly, the city guards. Years under the command of a cruel, ruthless overlord had rubbed off on some guards, while others had managed to maintain their humanity. I started compiling a mental list of who was who. Now and then, I would pull one aside for a quick word, including the guard who'd manhandled the boy earlier. Grove was the man's name.

"We're here to maintain law and order, aren't we, Grove?"

He nodded as if that was what he'd been doing all along. "Yes, sir!"

"That means protecting the townsfolk, Grove."

He saluted proudly. "Yes, sir!"

I took a deep breath. He didn't get it, did he?

"That includes the children, Grove."

His expression went blank. "The children?"

"Yes, the children. Women too."

His brow furrowed. Clearly, that was a new concept for the man — to protect rather than to take advantage.

"We have to be... nice, sir?" His voice was full of doubt.

"Respectful would be a good start. Not everyone is a criminal, you know."

He kicked the ground, not uttering a word.

"Innocent until proven guilty. Right, Grove?"

His expression was dark, and all he uttered was a glum, "Yes, sir."

I dismissed him, releasing enough of my dragon to make sure he felt the burn of my eyes on his back, letting him know I would be watching him closely.

Of course, I was careful not to let enough of my dragon out to arouse suspicion. The world was a dangerous place, and humans had a way of blaming all their woes on... well, anyone but themselves. Witches were burned at the stake, and wolves had nearly been hunted to extinction — ordinary wolves caught in a wave of panic about werewolves. If only humans knew that many shifters worked to protect them! Most of the country's bravest knights were shifters, along with some of the nobility. And yet one whisper of *dragon* was enough to send folks screaming.

If only they knew their hero, Saint George, who really had slain an evil dragon, was actually a shifter.

My dragon grumbled. *Another story they got all wrong. Stupid humans.*

Then a loud, high-pitched squawk broke out, reminding me of exotic birds I'd seen in the Holy Land. I winced, turning.

It was the two noblewomen whose carriage I'd intercepted in the forest. Now, they trotted up, as fluttery and excited as a couple of peacocks.

"Sheriff! Oh, Sheriff! You're wonderful!"

I blinked. Was I?

"My ring!" The first woman held it up.

"My brooch!" the second declared. "We're so grateful!"

So grateful, they practically threw themselves at me.

Be grateful to Robynne, I nearly said, backing away while they chattered about my bravery and the returned jewelry. They didn't mention the stolen money, which proved Robynne's point. Money meant little to the rich.

To the poor, however, it meant survival for another day. Out of the corner of my eye, I watched a woman hug her daughter tightly. She kept her right hand clamped over her pocket, concealing the coin she must have found. That coin could feed the family for a week.

Meanwhile, the noblewomen gushed with praises I didn't deserve.

"Our hero! How can we ever repay you?"

They fluttered their eyelashes and pressed close enough to suggest one way they might.

"Not at all, ladies, not at all." I did my best to extricate myself gently instead of pushing them away in disgust. There was only one woman I wanted in my bed, and that was Robynne.

"I knew that Robin Hood had a good heart," the second sighed dreamily.

The other frowned. "Wasn't it Robert?"

I rolled my eyes. That fool?

"No, Robin," the first declared, proving herself to be a good match for Robert in terms of intellect. "Robin Hood, gentleman outlaw," she declared.

A passing milkmaid's stride hitched, and in no time, the words had spread like wildfire.

"Robin Hood! Robin Hood!" villagers whispered in awe for the rest of the day.

I shook my head, but I couldn't exactly blurt, *You mean Robynne, the woman. She's the one to thank, not her idiot brother.*

But it was already spinning out of hand. The only thing not exaggerated was Robynne's skill with a bow, once word of her arrow-through-the-ring trick got around.

"Where on earth did he learn that?"

She, not he. And she learned from her father, part of me burned to blurt.

My dragon grinned. *The advantage of having an armorer for a father.*

A nostalgic smile played at my lips. Robynne had taken up swordplay at the tender age of three and archery at five. My father, the stable master, worked near hers, so Robynne and I had spent all day, every day watching them train the local lord's latest recruits. Well, we watched at first. Then we practiced alongside the others and eventually stood out as two of the best.

Not just two of the best, my dragon corrected. *We were the very best.*

One side of my mouth rose in a grin, thinking back on those days. The other side fell as I considered Robin Hood's burgeoning reputation. Especially since the tales spinning through town were just the beginning of what I feared might someday come to an ugly end.

Why? Because the noblewomen continued toward London the next day, no doubt jabbering the whole way about Robin Hood, the dashing bandit of Sherwood Forest.

Second, because the pattern repeated itself over the next few weeks. Most travelers detoured around the deep, dark woods, but those who were impatient or reckless enough to follow the King's Way through Sherwood Forest arrived at the city gates with a lighter load than what they'd started with.

"Bandits! Thieves!"

The men would bluster, the women would sigh and fan themselves. And each time, the legend of Robin Hood grew.

"Something has to be done," Giles, the captain of the guard, muttered when the fourth such party stumbled into town.

He was right. It was getting to the point where villagers started eagerly anticipating little treasures that might be left around town.

But as sheriff, I couldn't exactly endorse that.

To make matters worse, crafty folks started watching the city gates like hawks. They'd already dragged an innocent cooper from his wagon and riffled through his goods for treasure, thinking he might be Robin Hood in disguise.

The danger grew for Robynne every time, as well as for me. I was only acting sheriff — a temporary fill-in until a permanent appointment was made. That could take months or even years, especially with King Richard off crusading and his brother, Prince John, too busy with other matters.

My dragon growled. *Busy taxing and terrorizing the poor, you mean.*

If word got around that I was incompetent, a new sheriff would be appointed — perhaps one even crueler than the last. I could only alleviate conditions for the poor as long as I stayed in the job.

So, yes. Something had to be done. To protect the poor, and to protect Robynne.

The problem consumed me over the next days and weeks. Every morning, I reached across my too-empty bed, wishing for Robynne. All day, every day, I racked my mind for a solution. Every night, I paced my balcony, staring at Sherwood Forest.

Something had to be done. But what?

Meanwhile, I'd only gotten the briefest glimpses of Robynne, and it was killing me.

Staying in human form was killing me too.

Let me out. Now, my dragon raged. *No one will see. No one will know.*

I was so, so tempted. Even a knight's self-discipline had its limits.

Finally, on the night of the new moon, I snapped. Tossing my cloak and belt aside, I stripped, stepped to the railing of my balcony, and spread my arms wide.

Yes, my dragon rumbled, eager to be freed. *Yes...*

I jumped, too high and too recklessly. The wind pecked at my eyes and bare skin. Slate shingles formed an interlocking pattern on the rooftops below, daring me.

My laugh went low and growly as my neck stretched, along with my arms and body. One moment, I was a mere human, hurtling to certain death. The next...

Whoosh! I rolled and beat my wings. Flames built in my throat, and I nearly let out a jubilant blast of fire. Instead, I snapped my tail and headed straight up, like Icarus, though I rushed toward the stars, not the sun, on my own foolhardy mission. Only when the air grew thin and the lights of Nottingham distant did I level out and turn north.

There was nothing quite like the rush of beating powerful wings and stoking an inner fire. So much that I released a long, roaring flame.

My dragon crooned happily. *I am mighty. I am powerful. I am free.*

Then I glided along silently, which came with a different kind of high. My wings formed huge, stiff spans, letting the cool wind stream under me. I felt graceful as a dancer, agile as a kite. And when I swooped lower, skimming the treetops, I felt something else. My true love, calling to me.

Not the way she used to — by hollering from a treetop when we were both kids. And not the way she had when we'd gone from friends to lovers, beckoning me into her bed.

But call to me, Robynne did, because that's the way it was with mates. One soul sang to the other the way the sun sang to the moon. Reaching, yearning, calling to each other across vast voids of time and space.

Peering down, I thought I saw the pinprick of a fire. But the forest canopy was a tightly woven tapestry that protected its secrets well.

I closed my eyes, letting my heart guide me. My right wing dipped, and the air cooled as I crossed a gurgling river. Then instinct nudged my nose left, and when I opened my eyes. . .

Robynne, my dragon sang.

Her coppery fur glinted as she trotted up a rocky rise in fox form, popping in and out of the trees. I circled, desperate for a better look.

Desperate for more than a look, my dragon howled.

That, too, but I was willing to settle for less.

Come out, Robynne, I wanted to beg. *It's me.*

She emerged in a clearing, looked up, and sniffed the air.

One of her ears flicked, and her voice sounded in my mind. *You, the sheriff?*

I shook my head. *Just me. The real me. Daniel.*

She studied me a minute longer, tracing my circular path with slow, careful turns. When she whipped her tail and disappeared into the foliage, I nearly howled. But a moment later, she reappeared, heading for a high, exposed bluff. There, she sat, nose twitching as she tested the direction of the wind.

Of course, that wasn't as important to a fox shifter as it was to me. But as kids, she'd made me explain all the details of flying.

I grinned, thinking back on those times. Our animal sides had always been part of us, but, like most shifters, we couldn't actually change forms until puberty. I'd nearly died of jealousy when Robynne started shifting before me, and I'd spent months chasing her haplessly through the woods on two sore human feet.

I'd nearly died of desire, too, because shifting meant bare skin, and she was gorgeous, whichever body she chose. Trim, agile, and smooth, with modest curves in all the right places.

Back then, I had cursed at every branch that swatted my head and every thorn that pierced my thin human skin. The only dragoning I had been capable of then was spitting tiny sparks — not exactly the grand vision I'd once had of myself.

Then one night, intense pain had welled up inside, and when I cried out, Robynne trotted back to check on me, still in fox form.

Are you all right? she'd whimpered, licking my face.

I lay on the ground, pain racking my joints. I thought I was dying, but then I realized it was my dragon side, emerging for the very first time.

Wow, Robynne had breathed in awe when I finally transformed.

I'd held out my huge wings and stared too. *Wow.*

It was quite a rush, going from gangly teen to massive dragon in a single night, but my soaring ego came to a crashing halt — literally — when I tried flying.

It had been Robynne, jogging alongside me, yelling, *Now! Now! Take off!* that got me over the hump. Robynne believing in me. Robynne yipping in glee on my first real flight after too many painful failures.

Robynne cheering from below. Letting me become who I needed to be.

At the time, I had no idea how lucky I was to have her. Now, I did.

We used to spend entire nights exploring, her on the ground, me soaring overhead. Sometimes, we raced. Other times, we teased. Lots of times, we laughed. And gradually, we'd learned about other things — including what human bodies were useful for, like making love and holding each other afterward.

So many memories stirred as I glided around that bluff, I wondered if it was them holding me up in the sky instead of the wind. Then I blinked and looked down, in the present again.

Robynne sat on the bluff, quiet, unsure. Then she flicked her tail and took a step back. One, then another, and another, making space for me to land. Inviting me, albeit cautiously.

I circled again, then came in for landing. The trees and rocks blurred, because all I saw was Robynne, sitting on her haunches with one paw raised.

My mind blurred too, as if a witch were stirring time, mixing my past with my present in one big, bubbling cauldron. My heart beat wildly, because I knew exactly what would happen next. I would land, coming to a stop within a few steps. Then I would hold my wings wide, and Robynne would step forward.

I knew because we'd done that a hundred times in the past. Robynne would shift as she approached, coming boldly to two feet. All human. All bare, graceful curves. . .

In my mind's eye, I shifted as my wings closed around her, so we ended in a perfectly timed, tight embrace. Man to woman. Friend to friend. Mate to mate.

I would hold her close, breathing her in in a way I hadn't been able to in Nottingham. Then I would press closer and inhale her fresh, woodsy scent. I would slide my hands down to her rear and tug her close, connecting every inch of her to every inch of me.

I groaned in anticipation of Robynne nuzzling my cheek. Talk would come later, because we missed each other too much for words, and there was only one way to get acquainted again.

All that played out in an instant, and all in my mind. But the witch in my imagination must have cackled and splashed something into her magic broth, because it didn't turn out that way.

The bushes rustled, breaking me out of the magic spell. Robynne spun and reversed her shift, hiding her human features. Her growl and my roar echoed over the hills. Instead of landing, I shot over the trees, blasting air down with my wings. Whatever that was threatening Robynne, it was going to pay the price.

Growling, Robynne crouched, a ridge of copper hair spiking along her back. I peered intently. Was that a bear in the woods? A wolf? Worse, a human?

I was about to move in when Robynne sighed, recognizing whomever it was. She glanced up at me, calling off the alarm.

Just one of the guys, she grumbled.

Jealousy stabbed me, and I nearly smothered the intruder with fire.

One of the guys? my dragon roared.

For the next mindless moment, all I could do was rage. But my human side gradually wrestled back control. Robynne probably felt the same way about my living in the city, surrounded by female admirers willing to express their gratitude to the local sheriff in all kinds of inappropriate ways.

Sheriff... City... Laws...

Reality crushed in on me, and I nearly went after the beast in the woods, if only to work off some of my frustration. But those woods were Robynne's castle, and I wouldn't win her trust by torching them.

I circled once, twice, watching Robynne. Her tail drooped and her ears perked for any further alerts.

Then warmth spread through my chest, and I knew it was her, sending her love. Wishing, yearning, knowing the moment we'd nearly had was lost.

Not here. Not now. But someday, my mate, she assured me.

A cloud passed over the moon, casting a shadow over the landscape. Robynne shook herself and shot me one last, wistful look. Then she picked her way over the rocks and slipped into the woods. For the next few heartbeats, I caught glimpses of her copper fur. Soon, there was nothing but the chirp of crickets and the rustle of leaves in the wind.

I sucked in a long, steadying breath, then headed back to the city. That all-too-short encounter wasn't enough, but it would have to be — for now.

As I flew, my mind spun. It was time to look beyond myself, my mate, and that night. If I wanted a future with Robynne, I needed a long-range plan.

I flew back toward Nottingham, trying to do what I'd done in the Crusades: identify hurdles, expose hidden dangers, and root out potential enemies. But, Lord. There were so many of each. Where to start?

Seeing Robynne again. Soon, my dragon grumbled.

All right. But where? When? How?

All I knew was this: sooner or later, Robin Hood would strike again, and Robynne would share the loot with those who needed it most. But we both knew that dropping coins into the fountain in the market square wouldn't cut it. She needed a new delivery method, so to speak. And figuring that out was my best hope of getting close to her again.

The question was, what would that cunning she-fox think up next?

Chapter Six

ROBYNNE

Staring wistfully at the horizon was not something I usually did. I had more pride than that.

At least, I ought to. But being reunited with your soulmate after many long, lonely years had a way of messing with the mind, and I didn't have it in me to do much else.

How long I meandered after that I didn't know. Less than the lifetime it felt like, I suppose. More than an hour or two, judging by how far the constellations had wandered the next time I checked. It was the sight of Orion slumbering on his side that finally made me head back to my den.

Yes, my den. Robert and the others usually crowded into the rough shacks they'd constructed around the tree they'd dubbed Major Oak, but not me. Not after one sleepless night — my first in Sherwood Forest, months earlier — punctuated by snores, belches, and farts. Men! That and the lack of creature comforts made me conclude that resting in a den in fox form made more sense.

I searched the sky one last time, then trotted home and crept into my den. The outer part was half cave, half lean-to formed by a thicket. That area was big enough for me to stand in, with a few rough shelves and hooks to shelter my few possessions. The usual girl stuff: my bow, quiver, clothes, a spoon, my sword, daggers, various smaller weapons. . .

I used that outer area to shift into fox form, then ducked into the inner part of my den, a cozy little hollow deep in the heart of a bramble patch. Neither rain, snow, nor wind could follow me in there, and I usually slept like a log.

But that night, I didn't sleep a wink.

No matter how many times I turned in circles, no matter how well I fluffed my tail, no matter how tightly I closed my eyes, Daniel was still there. Only in my overactive mind, of course, which was probably a good thing. If he'd actually been there, I would have jumped his bones.

We belong together, my fox side mourned.

We did, but as my father used to remind me, life was complicated, and things were never as simple as we wanted them to be.

Which reminded me of my other issue — a more efficient way to dispose of the loot Robert and the men collected.

But it was hard to come up with a clever plan when most of my mind was entertaining wild fantasies of getting it on with Nottingham's hottest dragon shifter/sheriff. Okay, Nottingham's *only* dragon shifter/sheriff, but still...

I finally surrendered to sheer, burning need by shifting to human form and pretending the hands running over my body were his and not my own. Nowhere near as satisfying as the real thing, but it would have to tide me over until... until...

I bit my lip to cut off the thought, giving myself an artificial high. Pumping, pretending, wishing that touch were Daniel's. I held back a moan that was part pleasure, part sorrow, and finally shuddered in half-satisfying release. Afterward, I fell into an uneasy sleep.

The next morning, I woke up cranky, but even then, my mood went downhill fast.

"Look!" Robert announced gleefully when I'd roused myself to join the others. "The first catch of the day!"

He wasn't pointing to the trout John Little was frying for breakfast. No, Robert was pointing to the treasure heaped under the branches of Major Oak. Our two big mastiffs, George and Connie, stood to either side, guarding it proudly.

I balled my hands into fists, ready to punch my brother. He'd been riling me up since the day he was born — literally. I'd hated him then, because my mother died giving birth. On the other hand, she died so Robert could live, so I owed it to her to look after him.

But God, could I kill him at times like this.

"Oh, oh! How does this look?" Robert chuckled, holding gold earrings in place.

Alan jingled the necklaces hanging around his neck. "You'd look better if you had these."

Even Whitefoot, our shaggiest hound, had a bejeweled comb stuck between her fluffy ears.

I buried my face in my hands.

"Taking from the rich and giving to the poor was your idea." Robert's tone suggested *I* was the one driving *him* crazy.

"I never said to rob twice as many people as before!" I hollered. "Seriously — before breakfast?"

For a moment, the men hushed, surprised at my outburst. Then they exchanged looks that said, *She's probably just cranky because it's that time of month,* and went back to admiring their loot.

It only made me steam more. "How am I supposed to redistribute all that without getting caught?"

Robert grinned and pointed to John. "Tell her your idea."

I crossed my arms, too angry to speak.

"The way I see it, the sooner King Richard is freed from that prison he's being held in near Vienna, the sooner justice will return to this land," John began. "But we all know his no-good brother, Prince John, will never pay up."

I stirred the air with my hand. "So?"

"So, we start collecting the ransom ourselves."

Everyone nodded as if it were that simple. Still, the idea wasn't half bad.

On the other hand, it would take years to collect the astronomical sum of 150,000 marks. England's poorest couldn't wait that long for justice.

Eventually, we agreed to stockpile the most identifiable pieces of loot — jewelry and such — for the ransom, while distributing the coins to the poor. However, that did little to solve my dilemma — how to redistribute the wealth without getting caught?

Robert yawned. "Oh, you'll find a way. You always do."

If only I were the one with a capable older sister who could solve any problem.

"Just leave it by the river," Martin suggested.

Right, and let the next flood take it all away.

"Scatter it in the field outside the city walls," Alan tried. "You know, where the cattle graze."

I shook my head, picturing mud, filth, and cow pies.

Five equally impractical ideas came next, followed by a sixth from John.

"What about the church? Aren't they supposed to do good things?"

The men roared in laughter, as did I. "They're supposed to."

John's face fell until Robert chimed in. "What about Winslow Abbey?" He pointed in the direction of the monastery not far from where the river forked, five miles outside the city gates.

"Corrupt, all of them," old Christopher muttered.

John rubbed his beard. "That new fellow seems trustworthy enough."

Trustworthy enough for a bandit was not trustworthy enough for me, but when the rest of the day failed to inspire any better ideas, I found myself setting off for Winslow Abbey.

I stopped often to study the sky, wishing a dragon — *my* dragon — would happen to swoop by. But Daniel would never think of finding me on the way to the abbey, would he?

My fox wagged its tail hopefully. *What if he did?*

I had set off late — too late, really — and the sun was dipping low when I crested a rise and spotted the abbey. The outer walls formed a square, protecting the buildings within, from the lofty church to the abbot's house, cloisters, library, and so on, right down to the monks' cells. Only a handful of structures stood outside the walls, including the chapel I approached nervously. Not nervous from the prospect of being discovered by a monk, but by Him. God. I hadn't been in a church in years, and in the intervening time, I'd managed to rack up a fair list of sins. Most didn't seem like they ought to be sins, but I prepared mental arguments just in case.

Take gluttony, for instance. Life in Sherwood Forest could be lean, so our occasional feasts were balanced out by all the times we went to bed hungry, right?

I scratched my head, wondering if God kept tallies on such things.

Then there were the robberies I was an unwilling accessory to. That didn't count as greed, did it? Not when I passed the loot on to the poor.

Then came lust. And, yikes. Lately, there'd been a lot of that — but that was all Daniel's fault. Did that count as my sin or his?

Gingerly, I crossed the threshold into the chapel. Lightning didn't flash, nor did thunder boom, but my steps remained cautious as I moved farther inside.

Except for the rays of sunlight spearing through the west windows, it was dim inside. The sound of monks chanting vespers drifted in from the inner monastery. That, together with the sweet scent of wax, gave the chapel a somber, otherworldly feel. Which, I supposed, was the point.

I looked around, wondering how to proceed. Should I pile the loot on the altar, whisper a prayer, and beat a hasty retreat? Should I conceal the valuables somewhere, hoping they would eventually be discovered? Or should I—

A shoe scuffed behind me. I whirled, drawing my sword.

The metallic ring echoed through the space, and a man stuck up his hands.

"Oi. Wait. I come in peace."

I lowered my weapon, chastising myself. Oops. Just a monk.

Or maybe not, because other than the modest brown robe, the man looked every bit a knight. A handsome, golden-haired knight ready to sweep some fair, innocent maiden off her feet.

A good thing I was neither innocent nor a fair maiden — maidens didn't come armed to the teeth, like me — so I barely blinked. After all, I had my own knight/dragon shifter to dream about.

Knight... dragon shifter... and sheriff, my fox glumly reminded me.

Still, I couldn't help noticing that this man was too handsome for his own good — and definitely, *definitely* too handsome for a monk. Not my type, but ooh la la. How a nun could keep her mind out of the gutter with him around, I didn't know.

"Sorry," I murmured, sliding the sword back into its sheath.

He eyed it like a drunk eyes a drink as he passed by me. Then his nose wiggled, and his eyes went wide. Mine did too, because as clearly as my scent said *fox,* his said *lion.*

A young, handsome, lion shifter monk?

You don't see that every day, my fox murmured inside.

He continued silently to the altar, lighting more candles as he went. One took several tries, and his curse echoed through the church.

"Dammit!"

Then he froze, looking at the altar, then at me.

I grinned. "I won't tell if you won't tell."

He exhaled. "Thanks. Old habits die hard."

My ears perked. "You're new here?"

He sighed and plucked at his robe. "Yep. I'm a man of God now. Well, in theory. I'm still in training. Let's see how long I last."

I grinned. This man, I liked already.

"Let me guess," I ventured. "Third of three brothers?"

He nodded sadly. In the tradition of landed gentry, the first son inherited the family's title, land, and wealth. The second son was expected to glorify the family name by becoming a knight. Unlucky number three was destined for life in a monastery.

I looked the man over. A shame he hadn't been born second. *Knight* was definitely a better fit.

We exchanged sympathetic looks. As a woman, I'd had my life mapped out for me in a similar way. At least, it would have been, were it not for a few twists of fate.

Slowly, I reached into my pocket and pulled out a pouch, then loosened the string to give him a glimpse of the coins inside.

He whistled, and I nodded. Enough said.

I held it out. "I'd like to make a donation. An anonymous donation, if you know what I mean."

His eyes sparkled with the right kind of mischief. "I see."

That and the fact that he didn't grab for the money reassured me that I had the right man. A rich man, probably — or at least, one who'd been rich before being pressed into the clergy.

I pushed the pouch toward him, then drew it back. "But not for the church. It's for a better cause."

Oops. I halted at my faux pas, but he just chuckled.

"Trust me, I know what you mean." He motioned over his shoulder, toward the kitchen adjoining the chapel. "We feed the poor three times a week. A donation would allow us to buy more supplies and maybe even slip a coin into each loaf of bread. Good enough cause for you?"

I nodded. "Good start."

He grinned and went on. "Then there's the weekly mission to town. We visit the old, the infirm, the orphans' home..."

I gave him a thumbs-up, though I tapped my bow. "I'll be following up, of course."

He grinned. "Of course, Robin Hoo—" He stopped there, then corrected himself, "I mean, of course, Mistress Anonymous."

Oops. Was I that obvious?

I stuck to my sternest look. "As I said, I'll be following up. Are you up to the challenge?"

His smile grew. "It's just what I need to spice up my life." Then his gaze grew wistful, as though nothing would ever be enough to spice up a monastic life.

For a moment, I was tempted to invite him to join us in the woods. But, no. Clearly, this man was a dutiful son, and I respected that. Plus, if this arrangement worked out, I needed him exactly where he was.

Still, I held the coins back. "What will you tell the abbot?"

He winked. "Tell the abbot what? I'll keep it between me and the cook."

"And if the cook asks...?"

He shrugged and pointed to the altar. "Nothing like a good miracle from time to time."

I stifled a laugh and handed over the first pouch, then the other two I carried. Finally, I held out my hand. "Glad to meet you, Friar..."

He stuck the pouches under his elbow and extended a hand. "Tuck."

"Nice to meet you, Friar Tuck." I grinned as we shook, then stepped apart.

He touched his brow as if to doff a hat. "Nice to meet you, Anonymous."

Once he concealed the pouches under his robe, we moved toward the open chapel doors. My step was light and my mood upbeat for the first time that day. With my mission complete, I could head home.

Then a shadow fell across the doorway, and I reached for my sword. A tall, armed figure loomed, backlit by the slanting sun. Then I made out the man's features, and my heart raced in a whole different way.

"Daniel?" The whisper barely made it past my lips.

Robynne. He didn't actually make a sound, but his eyes sparkled the way they used to when we lay in bed.

"Ah, the sheriff." The monk's voice filled with venom when he recognized the thick chain necklace Daniel wore as a mark of his office.

Definitely a man I would trust, that Tuck, if he was as disgusted at the sheriff's reputation as I was.

Daniel growled back. "*Acting* sheriff. Have we met?"

"No, but I've heard about you," Tuck rumbled.

Daniel's features took on that exasperated expression I'd caught before, and the defenses around my heart slipped a tiny bit.

"Acting sheriff," I echoed, nodding for Tuck to go. "Not the one you heard about."

His eyes narrowed in a question. *Are you sure?*

I nodded, though Tuck didn't move for a full minute. He just stood there, giving Daniel the evil eye. When he finally stepped outside, Tuck bumped Daniel's shoulder — and not by accident.

But, oops. That made the coins hidden in Tuck's robes clink. We both froze, then stuck on innocent smiles.

Heavy silence fell, and Daniel's eyes bored into me while Tuck beat a hasty retreat.

"Here to make a donation?" Daniel finally growled.

I crossed my arms. "Just getting to know the neighbors."

I peeked behind him, checking for soldiers, but there were none.

So, Daniel had come alone, like me. Good idea? Bad idea? And if so, for which of us?

"What brings you here, Sheriff?" I asked, turning on as much sass as I could muster.

Daniel's tempest-blue eyes bored into mine, and an eternity later, he whispered, "You."

Chapter Seven

DANIEL

Puffs of steam escaped my nose in the chilly autumn air. My dragon was close to breaking out at the sight of Robynne alone with another man. A lion shifter, no less!

My woman, my dragon roared. *My mate!*

I sent a wisp of sulfurous dragon breath his way, watching until the lion sauntered around a corner and out of sight.

It had been a long time since so many emotions had broiled inside me. Anger. Jealousy. Even a tiny bit of respect, because the lion hadn't shown fear, and his first instinct had been to protect Robynne.

On the other hand, the clinking coins made him Robynne's accomplice and, thus, my enemy. Then again, being sheriff made Robynne my enemy too.

Feeling conflicted? Yes. More than a little.

Because *I* wanted to be that accomplice. *I* wanted to hold clandestine meetings with my mate. *I* wanted that trust, that common cause. Most of all, I wanted to kill my predecessor, whose brutal reputation cursed me wherever I went.

I took a deep breath, trying to calm down and think.

Trying. Not succeeding. Because a few growly words escaped my throat, along with a hint of fire and ash.

"Who was that?" I jerked my thumb in the direction of the lion shifter.

Robynne gave me that exasperated look usually reserved for her fool of a brother, and that hurt.

"He's a monk, Daniel."

I snorted. "That man is no more a monk than I am the previous sheriff of Nottingham."

She softened a tiny bit. "Well, some things you can't change. He's stuck being a monk. You're stuck being sheriff. I've been declared an outlaw."

I gave her that sheriff look I'd been practicing. "For the crime of...?"

Her crossed arms and deadly expression told me that was a secret she would never reveal.

Never? my dragon asked, hurt all over again.

Then she pointed at me. "You could have turned down the job, you know."

I snorted. "The way you could have turned down the chance to do the right thing with Robert's loot."

Touché, her scowl admitted.

I clicked my jaw and turned my anger back to the monk. "Whoever he is, I don't trust him."

Robynne made a face. "What about trusting me?"

Of course I trust you, was my first instinct. But five long, hard years in foreign lands had ground the trust right out of me. I'd thought that would fade when I returned home, but no. The way things were going, trust had become just as precious a commodity here as it had been in war.

Our eyes were locked, and I could see the same troubles occupying Robynne's mind.

Then my soul warmed the way it only did around my mate, and that hard edge softened again. "If we can't trust each other, Robynne, we can't trust anyone."

Her chest rose and fell before she answered in a whisper. "I want to trust you. I do trust you, Daniel. But the sheriff part..."

I clenched my jaw. "You know that wasn't me. That would never be me."

Her gaze wavered, and I knew she wanted to believe. But she was cautious, too — something I ought to have been grateful for. Robynne had to protect herself, even from me.

The thought cut my heart, though.

"I want what you want, Robynne."

She studied me closely. "And what is that?"

Us, I nearly said, and that was the truth. I wanted us to act on the promise we'd made when I'd left — that we would find each other again and spend the rest of our days together.

Unfortunately, those days weren't in sight — yet.

So, instead of saying, *Us. I want us,* I went to the other goal we both shared.

"Justice. Peace. A better life for those who struggle the most."

Her amber eyes heated to a fiery glow. "I do that by giving to the poor. How do you help?"

Exactly the question I'd asked myself, because helping the poor wasn't exactly in my job description. But I couldn't stand by and do nothing.

"I hold the guards back when they go too far. I've called off the most brutal punishments."

She flapped a hand, unimpressed. "That's simply not being cruel. What do you do to actually help?"

I rocked on my heels, considering how much to reveal. The more I told her, the more I risked myself. But if I wanted Robynne to trust me, I had to trust her.

"I've put a moratorium on torture and physical punishments. I've extended deadlines for outstanding taxes. I've clamped down on the guards' conduct..."

She didn't look impressed, so I had to aim closer to home.

"I help you," I hissed, keeping my voice low.

Her eyebrows shot up. "Right. Help."

Her voice dripped with skepticism, and I clenched my fists. If only she knew.

So, tell her, my dragon rumbled. *Make her understand.*

"I help any way I can," I finally said. "Why do you suppose I post the laziest guards to the city gates on market days?"

She opened her mouth to protest, then frowned.

"The very days Robin Hood sneaks into town to... What do the townsfolk call it? Ah, yes. *Redistribute the wealth.* Those are the days I post the weakest guards."

I paused, letting my words sink in. Then, seeing her unconvinced, I hurried on.

"That time half the guards were called away to check on a report of fire in the smithy — exactly when the tailor's wife was about to stumble across a little treasure..."

Robynne frowned. "There was no fire in the smithy."

"No, there wasn't." I held her gaze, willing her to understand.

The tailor's wife was the chattiest, loudest woman in town, and she would have cried out upon finding the coin — the first of many Robynne had scattered around the market that day.

The tailor's wife did cry out when she found the coin, my dragon sighed.

Of course she did. But the remaining guards were sufficiently distracted, and her husband shushed her quickly. Thus, no guards came rushing in to confiscate the loot, and villagers could quietly pocket any treasures they found. I knew. I'd been watching from the windows of my office above the square. Windows I left unwashed to remain as inconspicuous as possible.

Robynne stared, slowly putting it together.

Now that I had a little momentum, I went on. "Did you notice how few guards were around last Wednesday?" Then I grinned. "Clever of you to come in that day, by the way. No market, but with the tinker making his rounds..."

She stared with an expression that said, *Wait. You saw me?*

Of course, I'd seen her. No one else had — Robynne was far too clever for that — but I could sense my mate a mile away.

"There were so few guards because I posted my best men to cover the river crossing after a tip-off that Robin Hood would be meeting his secret informant there."

"*His* secret informant?" Robynne scowled. "What secret informant? And wait. What tip-off?"

I grinned smugly. "A very serious tip-off from a very reliable source who reported to the sheriff personally."

Her eyes studied mine, and I wished I could laugh at that little ruse I'd engineered. Of course, there hadn't been a tip-off or an informant. But no one had to know that.

No one but Robynne, who needed to know the truth about me. I wasn't that bastard, the previous sheriff. I was me, doing the best I could within the confines of my job.

In that way, Robynne had it easy. Robbing in the forest when the opportunity arose, sneaking into town to redistribute the wealth... She could do anything she wanted, when she wanted, including slipping away to conceal herself.

Me? I had nowhere to run, nowhere to hide. Whatever I did to help Robynne, I had to pull off under the watchful eyes of the townsfolk and the captain of the guard. I had barely an inch of wiggle room in any direction, while Robynne had miles.

But anything I could do to protect her — and anything to help the people I served — I would.

Robynne stared at me for a long time, then gradually regained her sass.

"So, you've been aiding and abetting an outlaw?"

I gestured the way the young friar had gone. "We can't seem to help it. Not when the outlaw has such a just cause."

Her throat bobbed, and the moment stretched. "Just cause, huh?"

I nodded slowly, whispering, "If only I could convince her I'm on her side." I let a heartbeat tick by, then winked. "Or should I say, *his* side? Everyone is convinced a man is at the heart of this."

Robynne grumbled. "Of course. Because men are so clever and women so terribly frail."

I chuckled. "Neither is true, and you know it."

Her eyes bored into me. "You do too."

I held her gaze. Yes, I knew her secret. And no, I would never tell. But what would it take for her to believe me?

The wind pushed a dozen leaves into the chapel, and they swirled, then came to rest. Robynne peered over my shoulder, grimacing at the outside world. Then she took my hand and led me to an alcove away from the door. Crucifix-size candles cast shadows over the wall, where a saint gazed sadly down from a painting. We stood there, hands clasped, eyes locked.

"I'll make you a deal," she finally said.

I braced myself, because Robynne had a way of thinking big.

She tapped my chest, stirring all kinds of primal instincts. "You stop collecting taxes on the poor, and we'll stop robbing the rich."

I shook my head. "Those taxes are imposed by Prince John, and it's my job to collect them." Her eyes flashed, but I went on before she could protest. "Now, how thoroughly I collect them..."

I trailed off, letting her fill in that blank.

"Is that all you can do?"

Heat rushed to my cheeks. If she thought I was a coward...

"I do what I can, but I can't make it too obvious."

She gave me a look packed with a hundred suggestions. I stared back. Robynne was as clever as they came, and she would realize my limits more quickly than I could explain. Heck, she would probably think of a few I hadn't. I would do well to compare notes with her.

But business was the last thing I was interested in at that moment. Candles flickered, and incense burned. I doubted the clergy intended for the scent to arouse, but they probably hadn't considered dragons. The aroma intoxicated my animal side, slowing down my thoughts until I could only consider one thing.

My mate. How much I missed her, and how close she was.

I closed my eyes, silently begging her to see past my sheriff's collar to the man inside. I didn't dare touch her, because she was probably armed to the teeth. I just stood there, waiting. Hoping. Wishing.

But miracle of miracles — we were in a holy place, I suppose — she slipped into my arms a moment later, and I locked my arms around her, inhaling her woodsy scent.

"Daniel..." she whispered, running her hands over my back.

I missed you so much, the gesture said.

I knew, because mine was a mirror of hers.

I closed my eyes, willing that moment to stretch into an hour. A week. A year. Something — anything — to make up for the time we'd lost. Her body fit perfectly against mine, and our warmth was a shield, hiding us from the outside world.

My thoughts slowed, matching the pace of wax dripping down the candles all around us. Slow... Slow... Barely moving, yet leaving a mark, like the trail left by a snail.

Keeping my eyes shut tight, I focused on how my chest — and hers — rose and fell with each breath. And for that moment at least, the world was at peace, because I had my true love in my arms.

The candles were an inch lower by the time we sighed and looked at each other. Outside, insects started tuning up for their evening chorus, and a flock of geese honked overhead.

Robynne's gorgeous eyes — deep amber, like rich honey infused with sunshine — were swirling, revealing her shifter side. My eyes heated from a similar glow.

"We need to think of something," she murmured, eyes intent on me.

My heart swelled. Men I had faced impossible battles with often said *we* when they meant *you.* You *have to think of something.* You *have to find a way for us to survive.*

But when Robynne said *we*, she meant it, and I knew she would fight just as hard as me.

My dragon sighed. *How many more battles would we have won with Robynne on our side?*

Many. I had no doubt.

I pulled her hand to my heart. "Maybe we can start here. With trust."

She bit her lip, and her eyes grew misty — the rarest of sights. Then she forced a smile. "Trust, huh? I might have to test that."

I cringed, half expecting her to assign me the labors of Hercules. But Robynne surprised me by easing into a kiss. A marathon kiss, as it turned out, making my body heat. I slid my hand upward from her waist like I used to do, way back when. Kissing, touching, playing, loving...

"Ahem," someone grunted.

They might as well have kicked the door open in a way that went, *Bang!*

We jerked apart, glaring at the older monk who'd just walked in. Yes, glaring, as if this was our holy place and not his. And in a way, it was — at least the spark-filled space our bodies had started to create.

But the man was a champion scowler, and he reclaimed that space. He strode indignantly past us, muttering a prayer.

Robynne tugged me to the door. She paused on the threshold, where the cold, crisp night air mixed with the candle-scented air of the chapel.

"I have to go," she whispered. "And so do you."

She was right, but I hung on to her hands. "When will I see you again? Where?"

She flashed a little smile. "As an outlaw, I'll have to keep that secret. But we will meet again. I promise."

I shook my head, unsatisfied. "Meeting as friends or foes?"

I saw a clever reply alight in Robynne's mischievous eyes, but a moment later, they dimmed again, and she hesitated, then touched my cheek.

"Friends. I promise if you promise."

"I promise," I rushed to echo.

She nodded, then swallowed hard, backed away, and strode off into the night.

Chapter Eight

ROBYNNE

Letting Daniel depart for the Crusades five years earlier had been the hardest thing I'd ever done. But leaving him that evening in the monastery was just as hard, though in a different way.

We were older now. Wiser. More scarred, but still hopeful. And as deeply, desperately in love as before.

My inner fox wagged its tail eagerly. *So, when do we get him back? When does life get fun again?*

I wished I knew. Were clandestine meetings and stolen kisses the best we could ever hope for?

I mulled the question over as I shifted to fox form and trotted home.

I splashed through the river on the edge of the woods, and damn, was it cold. Fall was truly upon us, with winter coming quickly. I shook my fur on the far bank, feeling more alone than ever.

Then, *whoosh!* a shadow swept over the moon.

I ducked, then glanced up at the huge, dark dragon racing overhead. For a moment, I crouched, dumb struck. I'd seen Daniel a few nights ago on the bluff, but whew. My heart still hammered as if seeing his dragon for the very first time. Wolf, bear, and fox shifters were fairly plentiful, but it wasn't every day I saw a dragon fly by.

My dragon, my fox yipped happily.

And, wow. I always knew Daniel would mature into a mighty dragon. But, yikes. A dragon that magnificent?

His wings seemed as wide as an oak tree, and the hard plates of his chest were broader than I remembered. Moonlight glinted off his leathery hide, and a tiny lick of flame curled from his mouth. I grinned in spite of myself. The show-off.

Daniel circled and swooped overhead, never too near nor too far, seeing me safely home.

My heart warmed. Good old Daniel. He'd always played the honorable knight in our childhood games, and he'd grown into the real thing now.

I tried to play it cool, but my fox side was a simple, joyous soul, and I couldn't help prancing in circles and barking in glee.

Mate! my fox called, again and again.

A low, thunderous rumble was his crooned reply. *My mate. I never want to part from you again.*

In human form, I might have despaired. But my fox lived for the moment, and for those few, precious minutes, all I felt was glee.

Whoosh! Daniel glided closer, teasing me. I jumped up, pretending to nip at his tail.

Snippets of the past drifted through my mind. The way we used to play-wrestle as children... Then the time play-wrestling hadn't ended in laughter but rather, in a kiss, followed by utter confusion, because we were only teens.

Then the next time and the next, when we figured out what came after kissing and spent the night tangled in each other's arms. I thought of all the nights of exploration that followed, when we'd gradually discovered the difference between raw, instinctive sex and sheer, sensual dance.

And now...

I sighed. Now felt like a different life. But still, hope remained.

I followed the stream on foot while Daniel soared overhead. At some point, however, it was time for me to enter the densest part of the woods. Time to say goodbye.

I swallowed hard, looked up, then ducked into the forest, resolving to get it over quickly. But even as I continued running under the thick forest canopy, I could sense Daniel circling overhead. Eventually, though, I sensed him sigh and turn begrudgingly back to Nottingham.

Which was when it hit me for the first time. My life in the forest might be short on luxuries, but I lived wild and free. Daniel had a much harder challenge in town. Sheriff... Sympathizer... Shifter. So many facets of himself he had to conceal.

When I finally curled up in my den and closed my eyes, I dreamed of him. Of us. Of better days to come...

That night blessed me with deep, peaceful sleep. The kind where one moment, I was lying quietly, and the next, I woke to find dawn teasing me with pink and gold light. I lay there, relishing the rare pleasure of a solid night's sleep. Then my ear flicked, and every groggy sense leaped to full alert.

In a flash, I shifted, dressed, grabbed my bow, and ran to camp, where I halted with a curse.

"Robert? John? Alan?" I called.

Everyone was gone — except old Christopher, still snoring in his bed, and the camp dogs who milled around my legs snuffling. I petted them absently. They knew enough to keep out of trouble. Why couldn't men be as intelligent?

I cursed again. I'd slept so well — too well, maybe — that I wasn't my usual hour ahead of the men. I was an hour behind, and they were already tracking fresh prey in the woods. I could sense their thrill and anticipation.

I took off at a sprint, intent on stopping them. Stealing from the rich and giving to the poor was all well and good, but Daniel was right. We couldn't afford to earn a reputation for ourselves.

I scowled, blaming myself, then my brother, and even John Little, whose keen bear nose had probably been the first to sense intruders in our woods. A fairly big party of travelers, I decided, judging by the hush of the birds. When a doe rushed by, followed by her wide-eyed fawn, my disquiet grew. Those were no ordinary travelers out there, sneaking through the woods. That was a large, bold group.

I ran faster, risking the open road that wound through the oaks. I had to reach Robert and the others before they made a choice all of us would live — or die — to regret.

I barreled around a corner, heart pounding as much from the thump of approaching horses as from my sprint. The intruders were close — very close.

So were Robert and the Merry Men. I cut into the woods and screamed into their minds.

Don't! Stop! Wait!

My chest ached, imagining I was too late. But for once, it appeared my brother actually looked before he leaped.

Whoa, Robert murmured into everyone's minds. *That's a big group.*

Too big, I barked. *Too risky. Nobody move.*

With no time to join my brother up in the trees, I jumped behind a log and peeked through the foliage. First, I looked up, making sure the Merry Men were well concealed. Then I focused on the road, straining to hear and see.

The jingle of harnesses carried through the dead-silent woods first. Then the earth trembled with the thud of dozens of hooves. I sniffed, but the breeze was too weak to carry much scent. Just a mix of horse, leather, and a hint of chain mail oil.

Wait. Chain mail?

I stared as the first rider came into view. Not a nervous traveler or inexperienced guard as we'd grown used to over the past few weeks. This was an arrogant knight on a coal-black stallion, both moving like they ruled the place. The light that filtered through the trees glinted off the polished armor both wore. The horse flicked its tail, and its rider flared his nostrils, testing the air.

Shifter, I realized, in awe in spite of myself. That man was a shifter, for sure.

I glanced up, willing my men not to move, not even to breathe. Thick vines of holly wound around the trees, and a good thing, too. Our standing joke was that the sweet smell covered the men's body odor when the creek was too cold for a wash.

Well, we weren't joking now. Every man was taut as a bowstring, keeping perfectly still.

Knight and horse sauntered on. Armor as smooth and polished as theirs probably hadn't seen any real action, unlike the dents and rust I'd spotted that first day on Daniel's armor. Still, I had no doubt this knight was capable — and more than willing — of inflicting a hell of a lot of damage. His sharp spurs hinted as much, as did the cruel turn of his lips.

A long line of men appeared behind him, all armed and alert, despite the early hour. Professional soldiers marching toward Nottingham. My gut sank. Was Daniel in trouble? Was he already being replaced?

Or might that be a good thing?

My fox wagged its tail. *Then he can join us in the woods.*

Much as I loved the idea, I knew better. There was definitely trouble afoot. Big trouble.

Another man galloped up from the rear of the long line, calling out, "Sir Guy! Sir Guy!"

Everyone tensed, and Robert's surprise echoed in my head. *Sir Guy of Gisborne? That bastard?*

That rich, cocky bastard, John Little's growl said. *Prince John's right-hand man.*

Heading to Nottingham? Alan wondered.

My eyes swung to Sir Guy, then to the man who'd called out. My nostrils flared as he galloped up, keeping his horse's neck bent with a tight, cruel grip on the reins. I didn't catch many details other than the snobby tilt of his head and the scruff of his unruly beard. But one sniff of his cologne-slathered-over-sweat odor and my gut roiled.

That man, I knew. That man, I detested to the depths of my soul.

"Lord Ramage." Sir Guy didn't bother hiding his irritation. "Did I not warn you to conduct yourself quietly in these woods?" He eyed the trees — the wrong trees, thank goodness, because Martin had just slipped, and his boot slid in, then out of view. "These woods are full of treacherous thieves."

That's us, Robert whispered smugly into the Merry Men's minds.

They chuckled, at least in their thoughts, while I could only despair.

Lord Ramage — here? Now? I thought I'd seen the last of him, but fate must have decided to test me once more.

Ramage shrugged off Sir Guy's comment and gestured to the trees. "They wouldn't dare show their sorry, fearful necks."

Robert bristled, making a branch sway. *Fearful? Us?*

I shushed him as Ramage blustered on.

"And if they did, we would cut them all down to a man — if they can even call themselves men."

I scowled, tempted to cut in. *I don't call myself any such thing.*

I would have loved to see the surprise on their faces if we ambushed them, but Sir Guy's men outnumbered us, with armor and chain mail to our leather and wool. We only stood a chance against them in a precisely planned, perfectly executed ambush.

My fox sighed. Precise planning — make that, planning of any kind — was not Robert's forte, and as for perfectly executed. . .

Leaves fluttered overhead as one of the Merry Men suppressed a sneeze. I winced. Perfect execution was definitely out. Luckily, only the closest soldier looked around, then dismissed the sound.

Sir Guy and Lord Ramage rode onward, their voices fading under the noise of their troops.

Look at them, John Little cursed. *Riding all high and mighty. What gives them the right to cut through our woods?*

They have no right! the men heartily agreed.

Still, no one moved, each man keenly aware that this was not the time or place.

What do you think they're up to? Alan asked. *Just passing through Nottingham or here to cause trouble?*

I prayed for the former, but the feeling I'd woken with kept a tight grip on my soul.

Trouble, I murmured, watching Lord Ramage and Sir Guy ride side by side. *Trouble, for sure.*

Chapter Nine

DANIEL

The town guards alerted me to our visitors long before they arrived at Nottingham's gates.

"Two noblemen, sir, with forty or more guards."

I dismissed the messenger, then sighed and gave Charger a last few strokes with a soft brush. We'd been through a lot together, that horse and I, and even though we were no longer at war, I still sought out the peace of the stables and the calm of my trusty steed.

As usual, Charger tuned in to my every mood, and he huffed in my ear. I smiled and stroked his forelock.

Yes, the world was a mess, and Nottingham especially. But we would make it through together.

Then I sighed again, because in my mind, I was murmuring to Robynne too.

We'll make it through this together.

I kicked at the straw underfoot, then patted Charger.

"Where would I be without you, brother?"

Charger sniffed in good-natured reply and snapped up another mouthful of hay. He was amazing that way — calm, almost docile most of the time, but able to turn into a raging beast on the battlefield. Not literally, of course — Charger was a horse, not a shifter — but he was still one of a kind. Finding a horse that didn't panic at the scent of a dragon shifter was hard enough, and finding one with a warrior's heart was even harder.

"Do you miss the action?" I murmured as I swept the brush over his back one more time.

Charger munched happily, as if to say, *Not as much as I feared.*

I paused, wondering if I could say the same. My dragon had always had a restless soul, but that had grown even worse lately.

Need my mate, the beast grumbled.

I grimaced. I was working on that.

Work harder, the beast grunted.

Just then, Charger flicked an ear. A moment later, hoofbeats sounded over the cobblestones of town, and dozens of mounted men burst into the market square.

"Ah, our visitors," I muttered, glancing outside.

I saw swirls of color — London's finest dyes, no doubt — and the glint of armor. The pretty kind not meant for the battlefield.

Charger snorted and pawed the ground.

"You can say that again," I sighed at the feather adorning one steed's head.

Then another man cantered in on a black stallion, making the others whinny and stomp nervously. Horse and rider circled the others, then stopped. The stallion reared dramatically, while the rider raised his chin.

Look at us, they might as well have declared. *We are in charge here. We are in charge everywhere. Woe be the man who challenges our power.*

I gripped the stall door, resisting the urge to do exactly that. Charger rumbled and shook his head, clearly thinking along the same lines.

I sniffed the air, then realized the man was doing the same thing. So, he was a shifter too. A powerful one, like me, and a member of the nobility.

I snorted. That last part was nothing like me. Neither, hopefully, was his cruel, power-hungry expression.

The stallion came back to four feet and turned in place, letting the rider study the town. I took half a step back, glad for the barn smell covering my scent. His gaze passed right over me, accusing everyone he spotted of innumerable crimes. Sunlight glinted off his spurs as he scowled and barked at the portly man on another fine steed.

"Ready, Ramage?"

I frowned, trying to place the name and face.

"But, Sir Guy..." Ramage protested.

My breath caught. Sir Guy of Gisborne? Prince John's ruthless right-hand man?

Charger stomped, raring to take him on.

"I must go," Sir Guy announced. "The prince awaits in London." He looked around, unimpressed. "I'll leave this business to you."

I frowned. Business? What business?

Make sure you don't let me down, Sir Guy's cold stare warned Ramage. Then, with a last, disdainful look, Sir Guy galloped out of town. Half the soldiers followed, which would have been a relief if the other half hadn't remained, forming ranks behind Lord Ramage.

Everyone in town exhaled, and I swear, Ramage did too. As soon as Sir Guy was out of sight, Ramage touched his sword as if to announce, *I'm the boss now.*

Charger snorted. *You can pretend.*

Ramage leaped off his horse with a flourish, a move that might have been impressive if one gleaming boot hadn't landed in fresh chicken poo. His foot slid, and for one hopeful moment, I was sure he was going down. One of his men caught his arm, however, steadying him just in time.

"Too bad," the stableboy muttered, then slapped a hand over his mouth. He looked at me, turning white. "Sorry, sir. What I meant, sir, was... Well, I mean..."

I grinned. "You said exactly what I was thinking, Peters. Too bad."

He exhaled and flashed a weak smile.

That ought to have been my cue to stride out and greet the new arrivals. Still, I hung back, observing Ramage from the stable door. It never hurt to let a man's actions inform me about his character, rather than his words.

So far, however, neither impressed me.

"Do you know him, sir?" the stableboy asked.

"I know the type."

Another arrogant, entitled young lord, in other words, who liked to lay claim to everyone and everything.

And then it hit me. Ramage was the son of the lord who owned all the land west of Locksley, where Robynne and I had grown up. I'd seen him pass a few times, on his way to the feasts and parties the noble class threw. Every time, I'd shaken my head at what a spoiled, conceited brat he was.

Doesn't look like he's changed, my dragon grumbled.

I wondered if he would recognize me, but of course not. I was too low-class for him.

Make that, low class and a man, my dragon growled. *If you were a woman...*

I frowned, catching Ramage eyeing one of the market girls with a look that said, *I'll sample your wares later, if you know what I mean.*

It was Mary, the baker's daughter. The one too pretty for her own good.

Bile rose in my throat at the image of Ramage cornering her in an alley, dropping his pants, and ordering her to her knees.

Mary scurried away, and I fought the urge to throttle the man. Then Ramage snapped his fingers as if his men were so many dogs. "Bring me that rascal."

"Yes, sir." One of his men motioned to those at the back of his train.

"What's the meaning of this?" Giles, captain of the city guard, asked as a young man was dragged forward.

"What's the meaning of this?" Ramage's voice went shrill as he imitated the man's words. "The meaning, my good sir, is that I have captured that menace of an outlaw, Robin Hood."

Everyone in the market square went still, making it clear where their loyalties lay. Then they shook their heads and exhaled.

"Young Ben?" someone guffawed. "He'd be lucky to steal an egg from a chicken."

I frowned, recognizing the blacksmith's son. The teen was almost as tall and powerful as his father, but with all the intellect of a Norfolk ram.

Menace? Outlaw? I nearly broke out laughing. Ben?

The way Lord Ramage gestured at him was no joke, though.

"Yes, Robin Hood. I knew the moment I saw him with this." Ramage held up a coin.

Giles leaned in, frowning. "Um... sir? A silver penny?"

Lord Ramage looked at him, annoyed. "Do you know nothing?" He threw up his arms, making the frilly lace poking out from his sleeves flutter. "Just last week, my godson was robbed in Sherwood Forest." He tapped the coin. "Robbed of everything, including this coin. See that cross and the crescent moon?"

Giles, the villagers, and I all stared wordlessly. There had to be thousands of identical coins in circulation. And even if that particular one was part of the stolen loot, it didn't mean poor, slow-witted Ben was the culprit.

But Ramage was out for blood, and any blood would do.

"Right, then." Ramage pointed to the wood block beside the town stocks. "Off with his hand."

The crowd gasped, and even Giles protested. "But, sir—"

Ramage whirled, practically screaming. "It is the law, and the law must be followed!"

There was indeed such a law, but what about a trial?

And, whoa. Ramage's men were already forcing young Ben's arm over the wood stump while another lifted a battle-axe and took aim.

I bolted out of the stables, yelling for them to stop, but the hubbub of the villagers drowned me out.

"I'll do the honors." Ramage snatched the axe and raised it in a sloppy, amateurish motion. Still, the blade — and his target — were big enough that even he couldn't miss.

I sprinted toward him, cursing. Not only would Ramage punish an innocent man, his actions would set off a full-stage rebellion. Had he no sense whatsoever?

"Stop!" I yelled, pushing my way through the crowd. "Stop in the name of the sheriff!"

I drew close enough to see the sweat pour down poor Ben's pale, terrified features. The glow of blood lust in Ramage's eyes. The grimaces on the faces of the men who held the innocent victim.

"Stop!" I repeated, getting closer.

But not close enough, because Ramage started to heave the axe. The blade glinted at the zenith of his swing, marking that split second before gravity pulled it back down.

Then, *thwack!* Something zipped through the air, leaving Ramage's arm strangely suspended.

A woman screamed. Ramage grunted. The axe clattered to the ground behind him, and the nearest guards scattered. I stared, trying to make sense of it all.

Then I spotted the arrow.

The one pinning Ramage's sleeve to the frame of the town stocks. I turned toward its point of origin at the very moment the first villager whispered, "Robin Hood!"

A ripple went through the crowd, and a moment later, everyone broke out in jubilant cries. "Robin Hood! Robin Hood!"

Ramage's guards looked at their master, awaiting an order.

"It has to be," someone muttered. "Who else wields a bow with such accuracy?"

No one. And not just accurate, but also smart enough to warn Ramage without killing him.

Still, her action had stirred a hornet's nest, and we both knew it was about to explode.

Finally, I located her, and our eyes locked. She was on the far side of the square, dressed in a brown and green robe — the colors of the forest — with the hood pulled low over her face. I doubted anyone else had picked her out from the crowd, but she was my mate, and a sixth sense led me to her every time.

My heart thumped, and the ache permanently housed in my chest flared to twice its usual size.

Her throat bobbed, and she shuffled backward, then turned and disappeared down an alley.

"Get him!" Ramage yelled, struggling to free himself.

He probably hadn't spotted Robynne, but any fool could tell the direction the arrow had come from.

In the ensuing chaos, the crowd hustled young Ben to safety. All in all, it would have been comical, only it wasn't. Not with my mate closer than ever to being captured.

I rushed toward the east side of the square, followed by several guards.

"You and you, check that way." I motioned, sending them the wrong way. "And you two — that way. I'll check here." I rushed into the alley Robynne had disappeared down.

Behind me, Ramage yelled, "Lower the portcullis! Lock Robin Hood into the city!"

And dammit, the idiot guards obeyed, initiating the creaky process.

I sprinted, following gut instinct. There were a dozen ways through the rabbit warren of the city, and guessing would get me nowhere. My gut, however, led me directly to a familiar stairway. My stairway — the very place I'd found Robynne that first time we'd met in town.

And sure enough, there she stood in the shadows, unflappable as ever.

"Hello, Sheriff."

Her eyes flared, though, and her lips twitched.

God, what I would have given to kiss her.

"Robynne," I sighed.

"You sound like my father." She chuckled — yes, chuckled, even amid the din erupting throughout Nottingham.

"Close the gates! Close the gates!" We could hear the order go up all across the city.

For an instant, my mind went to the past, and I nearly smiled. Robynne had been a handful growing up. Her father, a widower, had done his best, but I recalled him sighing frequently. The one that said, *You, my dear, amaze me. But this time, you really have gone too far.*

As usual, I found myself torn between arresting and kissing her. I settled for another sigh. "What are you doing here?"

Robynne's eyes shot daggers in the direction of the market square. "I watched Ramage and his men from the forest. When I saw them grab Ben, I followed them here."

Ah, Robynne. Noble to a fault. Most men turned tail at the first sign of trouble. Robynne ran into it at full speed.

"Ramage is a fool." She spat the name.

I tilted my head, sensing some bitter encounter. "What happened?"

She made a face. "It's a long story."

Her glance down the alley propelled my mind back into action. I looked up the stairs, tempted to hide her in my own apartment. But with my luck, Fitzgibbon, that drunk of a steward, would come along and find her there.

"This way." I led her down the alley. The east gate wasn't far...

But no sooner had we darted around the last corner than the gate slammed closed. We quickly backtracked.

"The south gate?" Even Robynne was starting to look desperate.

I shook my head. "Too far. By the time we get there..."

We stood for a moment, stuck. Then Robynne looked up. "Across the rooftops...?"

Not a bad idea, so I led her back toward my apartment. But the city guards were everywhere now, and the noose was closing.

Then, out of nowhere, someone whispered.

"Psst. This way."

I glanced right, where a man beckoned. I blinked at his white shirt, white arm, and strangely white face for a moment before it clicked. The baker. The man was the local baker, dusted in flour. And at his side...

My breath caught at the sight of the dark-haired beauty. Mary, whom I'd released from service at the castle?

They motioned. "Come quickly!"

Robynne barreled forward, and I had no choice but to follow.

The moment we rushed in, footsteps sounded in the lane, and the baker slammed the door. A dozen alarms sounded in my mind, because this was madness. The baker could turn Robynne in. He could turn both of us in. I could picture it now — the two of us led away in shackles, with the local people hissing at me — the sheriff of Nottingham, caught in the act of helping a notorious outlaw.

But when the baker motioned us past the glowing ovens and out a back door, we followed. Our fortunes were in his hands now.

Several buildings crowded around a rear courtyard, leaning into one another like so many drunks. Their upper stories were wider than the ground floors, making them all appear to tilt forward. It looked like a dead end, but the baker pushed aside some crates to reveal a narrow passage in one corner. My shoulders would barely fit, even sideways. But Robynne...

"That way." The baker pointed.

Robynne peered down the dark, dank space. Clearly, the neighbors emptied their chamber pots back there. Worse, the passage ended in a sharp turn with no indication of what lay around the corner.

I touched Robynne's shoulder. There had to be a better way.

Soldiers hammered on the bakery door, and Mary rushed into the courtyard, looking ashen. "Father..."

The baker urged us forward. "Go! Quickly! The passage leads to a stream, and the stream flows under the city wall. It's low — very low — but you can crawl through." He indicated Robynne, then eyed me. "Her, I mean. Not you."

I started to protest, but he cut me off. "We used it as a shortcut as children. These days..." He touched his generous belly, then smacked my shoulder. "I would get stuck, and you would too."

"But..." I tried, though I knew it was hopeless.

The baker turned toward the pounding on the street-side door. Any minute now, the guards would break in.

"I'm going. You're staying." Robynne clasped my hands in both of hers, and for a moment, my soul lifted. She considered for a moment, then kissed me full on the mouth.

My eyes fluttered shut, and time halted, though my heart kept hammering, as did hers. I could feel it against my chest. Warmth and light infused me, like that soul-filling moment when the sun blazes out from behind thick clouds.

Slowly, gently, Robynne eased away. Her hazel-with-a-hint-of-yellow eyes shone as she brushed my cheek. "We need to talk."

I nearly laughed out loud. Boy, did we. But there was no time.

"Tomorrow evening." The baker had stepped away, but I still kept my voice to a whisper as my mind spun. Where?

Robynne nodded. "Sunset. Three Rivers Tavern. You know it?"

I'd heard of it — an out-of-the-way place five miles out of town.

"Is it safe?" I meant for her, but she just laughed out loud.

"For outlaws, yes. For sheriffs, on the other hand..." She tapped the chain looped around my shoulders.

The ironic thing was, the tavern was exactly my type of place before fate had thrown me into my current job.

"I'll go incognito, then."

She grinned. "Like everyone else in the place."

A crash sounded — the guards breaking through the bakery's street entrance. Robynne whirled and, with one last, cocky grin, hurried down the narrow passageway.

Follow her! Protect her! Take a stand! my dragon hollered.

It took everything I had to resist the urge. Instead, I shoved the crates in front of the passageway, straining to hear Robynne go. First came faint, muddy slurps as she hurried down the passageway, followed by lighter splashes through a stream. Then nothing.

My inner dragon mourned, then roared as a company of guards burst in. The first two men screeched to a halt upon seeing me, making the next two crash into them and curse.

I stood at full height and glared. "I've already checked here. Go back." I waved toward the street. "Quickly! The outlaw must have headed to the west gate."

The guards went white. Oops. Were my eyes glowing?

I huffed, then pointed. "Well, don't just stand there. Go. Go!"

They whirled, tripping over one another on the way out. I watched them go, then exhaled and glanced at the baker. A simple man who now held my future in his hands, because he knew my secret. The question was, would he snitch on the sheriff of Nottingham?

He glanced back at the street, then made a show of dusting flour off his hands.

"Well, thank you for checking, Sheriff. A good thing there are no outlaws here."

I let out the breath I'd been holding, then echoed his words. "Damn good thing."

"We'll be forever grateful, you know." His voice grew husky as he glanced at his daughter.

I tipped my head toward the courtyard. "As will I."

He nodded, and that was it. Two men exchanging silent promises and a healthy dose of respect.

Mary gazed toward the passage Robynne had escaped down. Her lips barely moved, but my keen shifter ears caught her whisper. "Robin Hood."

I cleared my throat. "Nonsense. Robin Hood is a man."

Mary looked from me to her father, who murmured with no expression whatsoever, "Of course."

Of course, I nearly echoed, though they were no fools.

Instead, I cleared my throat and left them with a little salute. "Good day."

"And you, Sheriff," the baker called.

I forced myself not to run until I'd turned a corner. Then I sprinted up the stairs to my apartment, burst onto the balcony and leaned out.

"Robynne..." I whispered, scanning the fields.

There, in the distance, a movement caught my eye.

Robynne! my dragon cried, spotting her copper pelt.

My heart thumped as I watched her, now in fox form, sprint for the woods.

"Mate," I whispered, partly in pride, partly in sorrow.

Only after she disappeared entirely did I compose myself and head back to the market square. The city was in an uproar, and I had an angry nobleman to deal with.

Well, I was angry too. It took everything I had not to throttle Lord Ramage when I reached him.

"Did you find him?" he demanded.

Her, I nearly growled. Instead, I shook my head.

He made a face and flicked a fleck of dust off his sleeve.

"You'll punish the boy, of course," he said in that bored, arrogant manner of his.

"I'll punish the guilty, all right," I growled.

"Good," Ramage yawned, not quite listening.

Much as he irked me — along with the task of calming the mood of the city — all I could focus on was one thing.

Tomorrow. Sunset. Three Rivers Tavern.

Just me and my destined mate.

Chapter Ten

ROBYNNE

Three Rivers Tavern, five miles from town and half a mile from the cover of the forest, was an edgy, neutral zone that toed a fine line between laws and outlaws. I'd never been especially keen to visit, but I practically raced over the evening of my rendezvous with Daniel.

The wind was whipping and leaves tumbling when I arrived, just ahead of a brewing storm. Rain couldn't be far behind, but I'd made it in time. Would Daniel make it too? Would he come at all?

Escaping my doubts — and the weather — I stepped into the warmth of the tavern, heading for a shadowy corner from which to observe the scene.

Men crowded one table where a hustler took bets for throws of the dice. Over by the crackling fireplace, a pair of musicians played a jaunty tune, one on the fiddle, the other on a flute. At the other end of the tavern, a raucous group of men and women laughed at dirty jokes. A creaky stairway led to rooms for rent by the night — or by the hour.

All in all, not a place for a lord or lady. But perfect for an outlaw. And therefore, perfect for me.

I grinned, feeling more like an outlaw than ever after my escape from Nottingham the previous day. The baker had been right — the passageway led to a stream that ducked under the city walls. A dirty stream, though not as bad as the filth I'd splashed through first. The trickiest part had been getting down on all fours to squeeze under the city walls. My bow had scraped the stonework above, and my belly practically dragged through the water.

Outside, I'd stripped, bundled up my clothes and bow, shifted, and run for the woods in fox form with the awkward bundle in my jaws. I only shifted back when I was on home turf, where I forced myself to scrub in the frigid pool we'd created near our camp.

But, hey. It had been an adventure, right?

All of it, actually — from the first day I'd joined my brother in Sherwood Forest. It was funny, thinking back on those early days. The pool was one of the first improvements I'd put the men to work on after joining their stinky little community. Things had certainly become more civilized since then. Still, I had to wonder who'd changed more — the Merry Men or me? The men had definitely raised their standards but, shoot. Was I on the opposite course?

I pushed those thoughts away and focused on the tavern instead. Over by the bar, two no-nonsense women poured drafts of ale, while an older man prepared one of two dishes on offer — a platter of bread, cheese, and sausage. I fingered the coins in my pocket, and my inner fox salivated as a waitress walked by with the second option — a steaming bowl of stew.

Maybe just this once. . .

Then I yanked my hand away. Whatever Robert stole from the rich, I gave to the poor. I wasn't supposed to spend it on myself.

I did my best to distract myself from hunger by eavesdropping on nearby guests. Robin Hood was the talk of the tavern, and it was all I could do not to laugh out loud.

"I saw it all! It was amazing!" one man exclaimed. "Robin Hood pinned Lord Ramage to the town stocks with four arrows, one for each arm and leg!"

Funny, how tall tales took the truth and multiplied it. Still, it was nice they thought me — er, Robin — capable of such things.

"The guards closed the north gate, but Robin Hood scaled the walls!" another said.

If I'd just sipped a drink, I would have spat it out laughing. Quite the opposite, actually.

Surreptitiously, I sniffed at my sleeve, then nodded in satisfaction. The scrubbing I'd given my clothes seemed to have worked.

That was the silly part — how self-conscious I suddenly was.

Well, Daniel is coming. My fox wagged its tail. *We want to look our best.*

Never in my life had I wanted to impress a man — not even Daniel. But now, I found myself checking my hair and straightening my dress.

Yes, a dress. It wasn't often that I wore one, but I did now — an overall-style frock that went with my favorite shirt. I'd left home with that, a spare pair of pants, and weapons — lots and lots of weapons. Because, hey, that's what a girl's luggage looks like when her father is the town armorer.

A pang went through me. Was he doing well? Would I ever see him again? If he knew what I was up to these days, would he still be proud of me?

Take care of Robert, my father had said throughout my childhood. *Watch that your brother doesn't get into trouble,* my father would say, then tap my nose. *And watch that you don't either.*

Doing my best, Father. I stared at my feet and sent him a silent message. *Doing my best, I promise.*

Every so often, the tavern door opened, admitting a slice of chilly night air along with a new customer. Every time it did, I held my breath and let my foolish heart hope. And every time, those hopes were dashed.

Still, I looked up the next time the door creaked open, and when I did...

My heart missed its next beat, and my cheeks warmed.

Daniel, my fox breathed.

Unlike the towering oaks of the forest or the four-story buildings of town, the doorway lent a sense of scale. Daniel had to duck to get through, and when he straightened again, everyone in the tavern stared. It wasn't every day a tall, handsome, black-cloaked knight — an honest-to-God, *just back from the Crusades, don't mess with me* knight — happened along.

Of course, as a dragon shifter, Daniel had a hell of a presence, even in human form.

Heads turned. The musicians broke off in mid-chord. The woman pouring a draft missed, spilling ale across the bar. Rain started tapping on the windows and roof exactly then, as if the weather had been holding back just for Daniel.

He pinned the place with one hard look, and just as quickly as they'd turned, people dropped their eyes again. He strode over to the bar, exchanged a word with the tavern keeper, then turned to study the crowd. Everyone else, he skimmed right over. But the moment his eyes found me, they halted, and a glow kindled deep inside them.

His lips moved while his dragon crooned in my mind.

Mate.

Loud as a drum, my heart thumped, and my fox whispered back.

Mate.

Words couldn't describe how good it felt to see him again — the real Daniel. My Daniel. Not the sheriff, nor the young man I'd bidden a teary goodbye to years before. Just Daniel. The real thing.

My true love, my fox hummed.

Pride made me think, *Drat, he's done it again* — spotting me when no one else had. Still, I was more elated than annoyed.

Something had shifted between us since the previous day. Trust, I suppose. And with that shift, the barriers around my heart crumbled, leaving nothing between us any more.

Well, nothing but the dozen or so tables and the crowded tavern floor. With every step Daniel took, people hurried out of the way. The tables would probably have shuffled away too, if they could have. A log in the massive hearth cracked and fell, releasing an explosion of sparks that echoed what was going on in my veins.

I stepped forward to meet him, standing as tall as I could. Once upon a time, I'd been the taller one, but Daniel had caught up by the time he hit seventeen. When he'd left for the Crusades, my eyes were about level with his nose. Now, it was more like his chin...his mouth...

His lips, my fox said with a sultry swipe of the tail.

Over by the hearth, the musicians picked up the tune where they'd broken off, and the three men at the nearest table hurried away, giving us space.

I looked up into Daniel's storm-cloud eyes, doing my best to stay cool.

"This is your idea of incognito?" I scolded.

He glanced down, frowning at the spot his sheriff's collar normally hung.

"Um...yes?"

I might have rolled my eyes, but my fox made me lean in instead. And, wow. He smelled good. Really good. Like a springtime meadow full of flowers. Had he cleaned up for me the way I'd cleaned up for him?

I motioned to the free table, and we both slid in. Had our human sides been entirely in control, we might have stopped at opposite sides of the table. But our lusty beasts made us slide all the way in until our elbows and legs brushed.

Daniel motioned to my dress. "And this is incognito for you, I suppose."

I flashed a sunny smile. "Yes, my good sir. Can't you see I'm just another farmer's daughter from around here?"

"And what would a farmer's daughter be looking for in a place like this?"

I shrugged. "Maybe a dashing, heroic knight, back from the Crusades?"

Daniel snorted. "She should watch out. They're not as dashing or heroic as they seem." A hint of bitterness tinged his voice, but then he forced a little smile and pointed to different parts of my dress. "Anyway, a farmer's daughter wouldn't come armed to the teeth."

I fluttered my eyelashes. "Armed? Me?"

"I see three hidden daggers — there, there, and there." He pointed.

I tsked. "You only see those three?"

He chuckled. "Right. Your father would have taught you to carry at least four."

I shook my head again. "That was when I was a kid. I'm bigger now — more space to conceal, you know."

His gaze dropped to my bodice, and I nearly laughed. I'd stuck a couple of socks in there — a legitimate disguise, given the criteria by which most men remembered women. Otherwise, I wouldn't have had enough there to conceal much. But, hey. That worked in my favor when it came to swordplay, archery, or running for my life — something I'd done far too often recently.

The thought must have clouded my eyes, because Daniel touched my hand and leaned in.

"Seriously. You're not afraid of being seen?"

I shrugged. "Robin Hood is a man, right?"

Daniel snorted. "Find me a man clever enough to do what you do."

I pointed at him. "Now you really sound like my father." Just as proud and just as exasperated.

My poor, dear dad, having to deal with a daughter like me.

Guilt washed over me, and I longed to go home and reassure him that everything was all right. Well, mostly all right. Other than the fact that I was a wanted man these days — and I wasn't even a man!

My fox sighed inside. *How will we ever explain?*

A waitress came over and leaned way, way over to wipe the table — a cheap excuse to offer Daniel a full view of her fleshy breasts.

"What can I get you, sir?"

He kept his eyes firmly on her face, earning him a bonus point. "A drink." He raised an eyebrow at me, and when I nodded, he corrected that to, "Two drinks and one of those platters, please."

She opened her mouth, no doubt to purr something like, *Anything you desire,* but I growled first.

"Two drinks. One platter." I nearly added *Now,* but I went for a firm "Thank you" instead.

She walked off, swinging her ass, not that Daniel looked. Another bonus point.

I studied him — well, I meant to, but a man at the next table cried, "Robin Hood!"

I flinched and reached for the dagger hidden up my sleeve.

"Robin Hood?" another man howled. "He would never fall for that!"

I relaxed a little. I hadn't been spotted. It was just that my alter ego had another admirer. I tilted my head, listening. Fall for what?

Apparently, for traps they speculated the sheriff — Daniel — might set to catch me.

"I'm telling you, an archery contest is the best idea. Just find the winner, and you'd find Robin Hood," a man proposed.

I rolled my eyes, and Daniel mouthed dryly, *How original.*

"I bet he could split another arrow with his own!" another fan gushed.

I could, but I was getting a little tired of the *he, he, he.* Did it not enter their minds Robin Hood could be a she?

No, it did not.

"Robin Hood is far too clever for that," another man sneered.

I flashed Daniel a smug smile.

"Then make the prize something irresistible, like the kiss of a beautiful lady," someone else suggested.

I stifled a laugh. *You'd have more luck making the prize a kiss from the sheriff.*

Daniel arched an eyebrow. Had he read my mind?

"The most beautiful lady in the land," one man decided. "You know... What's her name... " He rolled his hand, stuck.

"Maid Marian," four men supplied at the same time.

And drat him, Daniel mouthed the same name at the same time. I glared, but he just grinned.

Not my type, but I hear she's ravishing.

I growled, subtracting one of his bonus points. *She'd better not be your type.*

"Apparently, he whispers to his arrows," another man declared. "He can make them go around corners and such."

Daniel tilted his head in a question.

I rolled my eyes. "They're crazy."

"Are they?" he whispered. "You do have a witch for a mother."

I made a face. "Half witch. And I only whisper to my arrows sometimes."

He gave me that look — the one that said, *Come on. Do you or don't you?*

A question I'd always refused to answer. Did I have magic powers? No. Yes. Maybe?

Frankly, I wasn't sure. Mostly, my accuracy came down to a hell of a lot of practice. Still, some of my in-the-heat-of-the-moment shots were so good, they even impressed me. But if that was magic, it certainly wasn't conscious. I preferred to think that was my mother looking over me.

A little pang went through me. God, I missed her.

"How about when you shot at me?" Daniel persisted.

I huffed. "Don't need magic for a shot that easy." I took a long swig of my drink, wiped my lips with my sleeve, and slammed my mug back to the table. "And I'm not a *he*, dammit."

Daniel held a finger to his lips in warning. I muttered into my mug. The tavern guests went on in a similar vein for a while, making Daniel more morose with every crazy scheme.

"I can't help it if Robin Hood is the talk of the tavern," I whispered.

"*You're* the talk of the tavern. It's dangerous, Robynne."

I knew that, and he knew that. The question was, what to do about it?

I mulled that over until the food and drink arrived. I made quick work of both, then took a coin from my pocket, tempted to order more. A moment later, I stuck it back.

Daniel followed the gesture, then signaled to the waitress for a second platter. I protested, but it was too late.

"My treat. I know you're too honest to use that for your own good. But even robbers have business expenses."

I frowned, picturing the sheriff's collar. "Is that what this is? Business?"

He shook his head immediately. "No." Then he frowned. "Well, yes, in a way. But..." He hemmed and hawed for a while, then tossed up his hands. "With you, everything gets mixed up."

A good thing the second platter arrived then, because what would I say to that?

I devoured the food, practically groaning at every bite.

Daniel lifted one eyebrow in one of those sinfully sexy gestures he was totally unaware of. But I was, especially now that my hunger had been satisfied.

Hunger is just one kind of appetite, my fox hummed lustily.

"Not such good cooking in the forest?" Daniel ventured.

I shook my head. Sadly, no.

Outside, the rain went from pattering to pelting, making it easy — too easy — to feel safe inside.

Daniel watched me silently, then motioned around. "Do you miss it? The easy town life?"

The fact that I had to consider probably gave me away, but I still tried to explain. "I suppose I miss some things." I pointed up. "A solid roof has its advantages. And I miss cheese and sweet rolls. We eat a lot of meat. But is giving up a few luxuries worth the freedom I gain? Absolutely."

I half expected a speech, but Daniel didn't utter a word. I went back to licking my fingers, because the food had been that good. That, or I really had been living in the forest for too long.

When I caught Daniel watching me, I blushed. Oops. Had my manners deteriorated that much?

Then I did a double take, because Daniel's eyes had taken on a soft glow, and he was looking at me in a totally different way. Watching my fingers. My lips. My tongue...

Heat inside me flared the way it had when we'd last kissed. That had been the previous day, when I'd been on the run. But now...

My fox hummed. *We have all the time in the world. And there are rooms for rent upstairs...*

I gulped my ale, forcing myself to think. Was I ready to go that far?

Yes, my fox practically yelled. *Yes!*

Still, I had to be mindful of the risk. A risk to us both, because if anyone discovered us together...

Together, my fox echoed in a sultry tone.

My body heated as if we were already naked and tangled under the sheets.

And, yikes. It was one thing to fantasize about sex with my hard, hot knight. But when the idea of sheets held its own appeal... I really had been in the woods too long.

The glow in Daniel's eyes intensified, and I knew he was thinking the same thing. Well, probably without the same fixation on sheets, but as for the rest...

I reached over and pulled his hood into place, then cupped his cheek.

"Your eyes..." I whispered, though that was a cheap excuse.

"*Your* eyes," he murmured, sliding his hands over my arms.

His dragon filled in the rest, whispering directly into my mind. *Your eyes remind me of who I once was, and who I might be again.*

The words had a tinge of sorrow that made me ache.

"You think you've changed so much?" I whispered. "Well, I don't. It's more like the world has changed — or maybe we just know better these days. We see that good and bad are more blurred than we thought, and we recognize ugly truths more clearly now."

"And what about truths we can't escape?" His voice was low, scratchy, and full of need.

I swallowed, because we'd inched closer. Close enough to kiss.

Like what? I let my eyes ask.

His throat bobbed. "Truths like, we belong together. Like destiny."

The word echoed in my mind the way church bells did when they struck midnight. Solemnly. Deeply. Irrevocably.

Destiny...

Years ago, the notion had thrilled me. It still did, but I was older and wiser now. Enough to feel fear as well. Because destiny didn't always lead to a happy end. Often, it led down a long, crooked path filled with obstacles impossible to foresee. Beyond all that was a bright, shiny prize, like the fountain of youth or the holy grail — a prize worth risking everything for, even if you knew the odds were slim.

A prize only a fool would venture to win.

My eyes slid shut as I leaned closer, then kissed Daniel long and deep. Because at that moment, I was the fool, and for my prize, I would risk everything.

Chapter Eleven

DANIEL

On my way to Three Rivers Tavern, I'd made a dozen resolutions to resist any temptations that might arise. But one kiss from Robynne — and one nudge from destiny — erased every one from my mind. All the sorrow of the past jumped on the bandwagon too, along with all the regrets and all the problems of the present.

All that, wiped away by one kiss. A kiss softer than any blow I'd taken on a battlefield, yet infinitely more powerful.

When Robynne drew away, it hurt as much as any war wound. Her words, on the other hand, were a salve.

"I missed you so much..."

I leaned my forehead against hers. "I missed you too. These last few days, more than ever."

Our *so near, yet so far* situation had been killing me, and I burned to end it forever. But how?

Another kiss followed the first, and when Robynne slid her hand along my thigh, my dragon roared for more.

Her kiss grew deeper, hungrier, until she broke off with a look of chagrin. "I'd hate to make the sheriff break the laws of decency..."

"I'm incognito, remember?"

She chuckled. "So, there's no one who can haul you away?"

I shook my head. "One of the few perks of the job. I can't arrest myself."

More heated kisses followed, and where our hands wandered, I'm too much of a gentleman to say.

Robynne leaned back with a tortured groan and glanced around. "I'm reminding myself not to draw attention but failing miserably."

I grinned and patted the key in my pocket. "Good thing I have a room upstairs."

Her expression went from surprise to delight, then consternation. "Are you saying you thought I was a sure thing?"

I laughed — too loud — then hushed and leaned in. "There's nothing sure about you, lass. But the city gates lock after dark, so I can't return until morning. Sheriff's orders."

She grinned. "All in the name of public safety, I suppose?"

I nodded, then rose. "And in the name of public safety..."

She chuckled, joining me. "...we ought to get somewhere private, *tout de suite*."

The words echoed her father's, spoken fondly, so long ago. And just like that, we were back in the past — the good part, where life and love had been so free and easy.

In no time, we were upstairs, careening toward my room like a couple of drunks. Progress was slow because we kept detouring along the way. First, I pinned Robynne against the right side of the corridor, squeezing the full length of my body against hers.

Full length, huh? Robynne teased as I ground my hips against hers.

I couldn't help it. And Robynne didn't seem to mind.

She *definitely* didn't mind, judging how she palmed that length next.

Eventually, we stumbled apart, intent on getting to the room. But a moment later, Robynne rammed me up against the other wall. Her kiss was deep and hungry, and our hands tangled. Then hers slid down my ass while mine cupped her breasts, and I nearly groaned. In a world so hard and rough, her soft flesh was heaven itself.

Soft? she protested in my mind.

Only in certain places. I squeezed her bicep in reassurance. Her arms were strong and wiry from drawing that powerful bow, running in fox form, chopping wood, and generally being the kick-ass she was.

Still, I quickly returned to my mission to reacquaint myself with Robynne's more secret places.

I dipped my head, desperate to strip her of her clothes. But, drat. Were we still in the hall? I was that far from caring about the outside world.

That way, you fool, my dragon boomed. *Tout de suite.*

I grinned behind my kiss, while Robynne just moaned.

"You promised me a room, Sheriff."

I stuck out my free hand — the other one was still exploring heaven — to point. "I did. But you keep ambushing me on the way."

"I'll have to take everything from you, I'm afraid," she sighed, nibbling her way down my neck. "Your sword, your money, these clothes..."

"Definitely the clothes," I breathed.

Her lips were too busy tracing my collarbone for her reply to be clear. When she dipped, my mind filled with visions of her on her knees, ready to transport me to heaven in a totally different way. But she shook herself a moment later and straightened with a sigh.

"Believe me, I'm tempted. But we really ought to get to the room first."

Which we finally did — in double time. The door thumping closed behind us was music to my ears.

No, music is this, my dragon corrected, tuning in to Robynne's eager moans.

I steered her from the door to the bed while she loosened the bodice of her dress, exposing the smooth curves of her collarbone...the creamy skin of her shoulder...her breasts...

The room was directly under the roof, and I couldn't tell which was louder — the pounding of the rain or the hammering of my heart.

I kissed my way lower and lower, and when I sealed my lips around her tight nipple, she arched halfway off the bed.

"Daniel..." she groaned, winding a leg around mine.

That worked — boy, did it work — for another few minutes of giddy foreplay that took me down memory lane. That night we'd made love in the loft of old Whittacker's barn with moonlight streaming through the chinks between the beams. Or that time we'd slipped away from May Day festivities to bond by a gurgling stream. Or that winter's night when our breath appeared in desperate puffs, marking each hard, hot thrust as our bodies joined.

Laughter broke out in the tavern below, and a horse whinnied in the distance. I jerked my head up, every nerve on alert.

Robynne smoothed her hands over my back. "Just the rain. The tavern. The night."

I hung my head, not wishing to admit how often that happened since I'd come home. That waking-up-in-a-cold-sweat feeling, thinking that an all-out battle was about to erupt. The shaky hands, the weary feet. The ultrasharp vision that couldn't stop searching for an invisible enemy.

"All good, my love." Robynne stroked my cheek.

Usually, it took an eternity for me to escape the void ugly memories dragged me to. But with Robynne, all it took was a few blinks.

"Nothing but the rain out there," she murmured in a soft, reassuring tone. "But in here..." Her voice dropped to a tease, and she touched her dress. It was down by her belly by then, and her twinkling eyes told me where she wanted it next.

Off, her fox chuckled. *All the way off, please. Tout de suite.*

She took my hands, helping me by hoisting her hips. I worked the dress off, tossed it over a chair, and turned back, ready to dive into a mind-numbing kiss. But the sight of Robynne laid out before me like a gift...

Lord, was she beautiful. And, sweet heaven. The glow in her eyes...

I paused, and for a moment, my inner inferno became the warm crackle of a fireplace.

Home, my soul sang. *I'm finally home, after so many years.*

"Now then," Robynne murmured, reaching for my shoulders.

Oops. I was still fully clad, if disheveled from our journey down the hall. Robynne sat up to make quick work of those last layers. Then we paused, Robynne lying back on the bed while

I knelt between her legs. Both of us soaked in the moment before rushing to the next level.

But when we did move — whew! Everything blurred, from Robynne's whispers to the rustle of crisp sheets. The heat of her body, the ache in my groin. The snug grip of Robynne's legs around my waist, the dip of my hips...

Then I was sliding into her tight, hot sheath and anchoring myself deep.

Robynne's moan was sharp, like the edge of pain we both felt. But a few heavy heartbeats later, when her body adjusted to mine...

"More..." she urged.

I pulled out, then thrust back in, and soon, we were moving in perfect time. Our bodies undulated with waves of pleasure. Waves that grew steeper and faster, not just rolling but crashing against the shore. Then a monster wave formed, lifting us both. I grabbed a quick breath, then thrust even deeper and hung on for the ride.

A ride of a lifetime, sending us tumbling. Then, with a satisfied swish, the wave subsided, leaving us both panting on a sandy shore.

Or rather, panting in the sheets, as I discovered when the blur gradually cleared. That wasn't a wild coastline, but the bed. The wind blasting around my body was a storm of emotions, not an ocean tempest. And that warm glow inside...

I went limp, holding Robynne close. That was satisfaction. The deepest, purest kind.

For a while, the only sound was the pounding rain over the roof, the murmur of voices from the tavern below, and our thumping hearts. Then Robynne sighed, stretched, and snuggled close. Her lips covered mine, lingering over every inch. I shut my eyes, cementing the moment into my mind.

That was one lesson I'd learned as a soldier — to cherish the good and lock it in a treasure box of memories. To keep it there for later, just in case.

"Oh my God, I've never felt this good," Robynne sighed.

I added that to my treasure box, fitting it among the most magical sunsets and the most beautiful vistas.

Then she laughed, and I opened my eyes.

She patted the space next to me. "Before this all goes to your head, half the pleasure comes from having a mattress."

I laughed and held her closer. "Half is fine with me."

The way she cuddled gave me credit for much more than half, and my dragon side glowed. But a moment later, I frowned.

"Wait. The mattress?"

She nodded, one finger absently tracing the lines of my abdomen. "I love the freedom of the forest, but it's not exactly luxury living."

My heart squeezed. I'd been too consumed by our sheriff/outlaw dilemma to consider the details of her life in the forest. But now... All the cold, wet, stony places I'd slept in on my way to the Holy Land came back to me. I knew all too well how slowly minutes passed in misery like that.

Robynne shrugged. "Good thing I'm a fox. I can just shift, curl up, and fluff my tail." She grinned and placed a finger across her nose, mimicking a tail. "It's very important to keep your nose warm."

I laughed. Dragons curled up in a similar way, though I preferred to tuck my head under my wing.

I closed my eyes, indulging in a fantasy of the two of us slumbering in animal form. Robynne could curl up in a furry ball under my wing, and I could wind my tail and neck around her body and watch over her.

The thought would have made me sigh in pleasure if I hadn't already been so happy.

Robynne raised her arms and pointed her toes, stretching to her full length. "The forest is fine, but lying in the bed... I missed it more than I realized."

I grinned, watching her smile at nothing in particular. Then her eyes slid to me, and her chest lifted with her next breath.

What? I nearly asked.

She likes what she sees, my dragon hummed lustily.

I was on my side, propped on one elbow, with the sheets somewhere down by my feet. Totally exposed — all of me. All the muscle, but all the scars too. Even a dragon didn't survive the Crusades without a few permanent blemishes.

But Robynne didn't look at the scars so much as past them, and her amber eyes took on a new glow.

She definitely likes what she sees, my dragon chuckled as her gaze dropped lower.

I winced at the rush of blood to my groin, and Robynne stifled a smile.

"Poor baby. Didn't mean to get you all worked up." She emphasized the last word.

I didn't move because, hell. When the love of your life likes the look of you, you wait.

"I like getting worked up," I admitted. "Five years is a long time to wait."

Robynne froze, and I cursed myself. Apparently, I'd said the wrong thing. But what?

"You... waited?" she finally whispered. "For me?"

I shrugged. "Who else would I wait for?"

Her throat bobbed, and her eyes glimmered with tears. Happy tears?

I touched her chin. "You're the only one for me, Robynne."

Her lips wavered. "You weren't even... tempted?"

I laughed. "Oh, I was definitely tempted."

Lord knew there had been times, especially the farther I'd gotten from home, when so many of the men made excuses about promises to loved ones at home. They were so far, so tired, so lonely... And loose company was easy to find, whether from women who sold their services — or were forced to by circumstance and some controlling scumbag. Other women gave themselves freely, seeing more *saint* than *sinner* in us soldiers. Maybe even hoping a bit of the former would brush off. After all, the Pope had proclaimed ours a righteous war and promised a place in heaven for those who died for a higher cause.

I'd set off believing that, but I'd come home jaded. No war was just, and heaven grew ever more distant when you witnessed — and inflicted — so much suffering.

I looked into the past, then back at Robynne.

"And yet you waited," she said, ever so quietly.

I shrugged, forcing a tight smile. "You know what they say about a true knight — as celibate as a monk."

Robynne snorted. "I have my doubts about monks. I bet they're more talk than action when it comes to celibacy. Or maybe too much action, if you know what I mean."

I laughed. "Well, I waited. And waited... But you know what? It was worth it — and not just for the mattress."

"You..." Robynne shook her head ruefully, as if she'd put up with my bad jokes for years. But the glow was back in her eyes, and when she dipped in for a kiss, it was hungry. Really hungry, as if she'd remembered she hadn't actually been putting up with me for years.

In no time, she'd pressed me flat on my back, kissing me feverishly, first on the mouth, then along my neck and chest. She dipped lower, kissing her way down my abs. My very hard abs, because now, every muscle in my body tensed, anticipating what she might do. Would she really...?

I hissed, closing my eyes as she sealed her lips over my hard, straining shaft. Perfect, bossy lips that ordered me to lie back and enjoy the ride.

Quite the challenge with a roaring, hungry dragon inside. But that was mostly for show, because the beast was as much of a pushover as I was when it came to our mate.

I lay there, whispering to her in little snippets of foreign languages I'd picked up while I'd been away — the good words, I mean. Special words that rolled melodically off the tongue when people marveled at delicious meals, stunning views, home, or their loved ones.

Robynne was singing, too — well, in my head, at least. Telling me to let go and enjoy.

Enjoy I did, as long as I could stand it. But the closer I edged to sweet, sweet release, the more I wanted to take Robynne there with me, especially now that I was really with my mate, instead of fumbling my way through another hollow fantasy.

Robynne must have felt the same, because she released me with a last, lusty lick, retraced her way to my mouth, and kissed me there. Then we rolled, and I took the top. In the space of three out-of-control heartbeats, we found the perfect position, and I plunged inside.

"Yes..." Robynne murmured, clutching my back and rear. Urging me on, telling me how good she felt, and begging for more, more, and more.

I needed more too. Nothing would erase the long years we'd been apart, but a bridge was stretching across that lonely chasm, connecting us more securely than ever before. When we both came, my vision exploded with swirling sparks and flames. The good kind, like a dragon breathing fire for sheer pleasure, then breaking off to watch the flames swirl toward the stars.

Long after the fireworks faded, heat tickled my soul, and I lay there, holding Robynne.

"Worth the wait." Robynne's whisper was a reminder that I wasn't the only one who'd been lonely.

I held my true love close — as close as I had in my dreams, all those years. "Worth the wait, my love."

Chapter Twelve

ROBYNNE

I woke slowly, reluctantly. My eyes remained tightly shut, blotting out sight while I savored every sensation. The warm, heavy weight of my mate, pressing over me. The sheer satisfaction of body and soul, crackling within me like a fireplace. The sweet scent of sex mixed with the fresh, leathery scent of dragon.

My dragon.

I held him closer and sighed.

Sometime in the night, the rain had ceased. Now, dawn was breaking, and I could feel its faint rays warming my back. Above that, I registered a gentle stroke — Daniel's callused fingers, tracing the lines of my shoulder blades.

A long time ago, my father, Robert, and I had a calico cat who loved to curl up in the sunny spot beside the front window in winter. Now, I knew exactly how she'd felt.

For a while, I lazed like that cat. Then a kiss on my shoulder made me smile and peek.

"Good morning," I whispered.

Daniel didn't answer right away. He finished the kiss first — a long, lingering kiss that spoke of lonely times not far enough in the past. Only then did he shake his head and murmur, "Not morning yet."

I chuckled as he kissed his way across my chest, secretly hoping he might scout his way right down to my core. Because those lips... that touch... the soft, wondrous gaze... Each made me want to clutch him and beg him to never, ever leave.

But that wasn't the reality of our situation, and I knew it.

Whether he read my thoughts or simply sensed my mood shift, I didn't know. All I knew was that he pulled back and nestled beside me, settling for more neutral ground.

He took a deep breath and spoke softly. "We have a lot of catching up to do."

The previous evening, I'd been eager to discuss so much. Now, I didn't even want to think. But Daniel was right — if not now, then when?

I clasped his hand. "I guess we do."

Daniel's eyes studied mine for a while, then went distant. "I have so many questions..."

I waited, dreading every one.

"What brought you to Sherwood Forest?" he finally began.

A nice way of asking, *What law did you break?*

I snorted. "A little altercation with that fool who rode into Nottingham yesterday — Ramage."

"Ramage?" His eyes sparked — and not in a good way.

I nodded begrudgingly. "Yes, Ramage. The man I was betrothed to after you left."

Daniel shot up in bed, and a lick of fire escaped his lips. "Betrothed?"

I reached for Daniel's hand, willing him to calm down. As touched as I was by his reaction, it really wouldn't do for him to torch the tavern — especially while we were naked in bed. I could already hear the town gossips...

Positively scandalous! The sheriff came stumbling out of the tavern, as bare as the day he was born, with some hussy, no less. I hear the flames weren't just from the burning building, if you know what I mean.

I sighed. I was no more a hussy than I was the male outlaw Robin Hood, but no one would care about details like that.

"Whoa there." I steadied him. "You know I would never accept any such betrothal — least of all, to the likes of him."

Still, Daniel's eyes sparked with outrage. "But... how? Why?"

"Exactly what I said when it all happened," I sighed. "Minus a few expletives."

Daniel looked like he might leap out of bed, gallop back to town, and throttle the man. A good thing he didn't know Ramage had tried to force himself on me.

Well, we showed him. My fox snickered at the memory of the well-placed kick that left Ramage rolling in the dirt, clutching his groin.

"Why Ramage, of all the fools who don't deserve you?" Daniel growled.

My soul warmed at his words, and I did my best to explain.

"I'd always been told my mother came to Locksley as a young widow when I was a baby. But it turns out that wasn't exactly true. She wasn't a widow. She'd fallen pregnant after a fling with a human, but she'd left when the man showed no interest in her or me."

Learning that hadn't bothered me much, because I'd grown up with a great father — the armorer of Locksley, who my mother had settled down with after I was born. Technically, that made my father a stepfather and Robert my half brother. But my family had never done things by halves, and we never would. For the same reason, it had never been an issue that my father and brother were both wolf shifters, while I was a fox from the mixed witch-shifter blood of my mother's side of the family.

Daniel didn't look bothered by that either, until I got to the punch line.

"Turns out the fling wasn't with just any man. It was the son of the lord of Barnum."

Daniel's eyes went wide at the mention of an estate near Locksley — one even bigger and with a wealthier lord than our own. When Lord Barnum died, his son was the last in the family line.

"No one ever cared about the connection — least of all me," I said. "At least, not until the younger Lord Barnum got himself killed in the Crusades."

Daniel snorted. "I heard about that. I wasn't far away at the time, actually. Apparently, he was stabbed by a prostitute he refused to pay."

"Well, they cleaned up the story by the time it worked its way home. Made him sound like a goddamned hero."

Daniel's eyes grew darker still, suggesting Barnum wasn't the only cowardly lord whose reputation had been embellished.

My heart twinged as I traced the scar on Daniel's side. My mate had survived countless battles, not from the safety of the rear, but by fighting on the front line. Brutally, no doubt — but honorably, unlike Barnum and his ilk.

I sighed. What my mother had seen in him, I couldn't imagine.

"But why Ramage?" Daniel asked, still flabbergasted.

I could relate to the sentiment. I had been just as shocked at the time.

"Why would a nobleman like Ramage take an interest in a commoner like me? He never did, and thank goodness. Can you imagine a worse fate?"

I let the question hang in the air as long as I could stomach it — not very long — and went on.

"But suddenly, I wasn't a commoner any more."

Daniel's eyes blazed. *There was never anything common about you, my love. Not then, not now.*

I kissed his knuckles, then went on. "Barnum the younger was the last in his line, and his death left the family with no heirs. There was only a distant cousin with no direct claim to the inheritance. But if that cousin could marry off his long-lost niece — me — in a favorable match..." I trailed off there.

Slowly, Daniel worked out the rest. "Barnum's cousin tracked you down and proposed you marry Ramage?"

He sounded as sick as I'd felt at the time. I'd gone from plain old, tomboy Robynne, daughter of the armorer — safely ignored by everyone — to a marriageable woman of noble lineage. Most of the village girls considered me lucky, but for me, it had been hell.

"Barnum's cousin didn't *propose* anything. He ordered it, and Ramage was happy to comply. Marriage into the Barnum line would double the land under his control — at least, as he saw it. I'm sure my long-lost relative had a different plan, however."

Daniel nodded slowly. "Like taking control while letting Ramage believe he had the authority."

I nodded. "After years of ignoring Barnum's illegitimate daughter — me — that cousin was desperate to have me recognized. To him, I was a breeding machine that could produce a new family heir — or two or three. Then he could get rid of Ramage and manipulate the children any way he wanted."

It sickened me to think of being used in such a way — and to see my children, if I ever actually had any, be manipulated too.

If ever we have children, it will only be with Daniel, my fox declared.

"Anyway," I finished, "I wanted nothing to do with Ramage, so I left."

It wasn't as simple as that, and the proud shine in Daniel's gaze told me knew it.

"You left — for Sherwood Forest?"

I nodded. "Robert was already here. I helped him leave a few months before all that blew up."

"What was his crime?"

I scowled. "About as sinister as any of the other men's crimes. Stealing bread — and not even for himself!" I sighed at the one honorable act my not-too-intelligent brother had ever pulled off. "For a girl he was in love with."

Daniel raised his eyebrows. "Robert in love with just one woman?"

I laughed. "Let's say, she was his true love of the week."

Daniel studied me for a while. "And you've been in Sherwood Forest ever since."

I nodded firmly. "Yes. A woman of noble lineage — that's me, believe it or not — hiding out among outlaws. Scandalous, eh? The ironic thing is, I feel freer there than I ever did, even at home."

Home. For the hundredth time, I realized how lucky I had been to grow up the way I had. I'd always missed my mother, but my father made up for that loss with boundless love, and he'd always given me free rein, no matter how much other folks disapproved.

I sighed and dropped back onto the mattress. "Anyway, Sherwood Forest is home now. And I love it — though I wouldn't mind sleeping like this more often."

Daniel chuckled. "Are you saying it was only the mattress that drew you here?"

I laughed, tracing a finger across his bare chest. "Well, there might have been a secondary attraction..."

"Secondary?" he protested.

With a chuckle, I slid my leg over his and rolled until I was straddling him. "I might need a little more time to reach my final verdict."

Daniel's eyes glowed. "A little more time, eh?"

His hands played over my hips, helping me find exactly the right spot. I nearly yowled when my soft core found his shaft, already hard and waiting for more.

I hummed, easing down over him. "Yes. I need a little more evidence before I decide."

"A little?" Daniel growled, pushing up to fill me.

I bit back a hiss of pleasure. God, was teasing fun.

My voice grew husky as I anchored my hands on either side of his shoulders and began to rock.

"A lot more evidence. That's what I need."

Need was truly the word — I needed Daniel desperately. The previous night had been a good start, but we had years to make up for.

"Then more is what you'll get," he vowed, pushing up again.

That was the last we said for a while, concentrating on the timing of each hard, hot slide instead. I found the perfect rhythm, driving down exactly as Daniel thrust up. Gradually, I leaned back, letting my head loll as I rode my lover.

"Yes..." I murmured again and again as my nerves wound steadily toward their peak.

Daniel's hold tightened and his eyes went to half-mast. Then, with a groan, he raised his head and leaned to one side.

"Hey!" I protested, losing balance. Although "losing" was relative, because when Daniel rolled to take the top and hammered back inside, I gained so much more — like a rush of ecstasy that overwhelmed every nerve.

Daniel thrust once. . . twice. . .

I braced in anticipation of number three, but instead, Daniel sucked in a deep breath and covered my mouth with his.

A kiss from my mate was always welcome, but honestly. At a time like this?

Then my eyes flew open, realizing what he had in mind.

A dragon kiss.

Whoosh! He exhaled, filling my lungs with fire. My body arched, and a thousand images burst into my mind. I saw the two of us intertwined, making love. I saw a landscape sweep beneath me, with the roofs of Nottingham, the endless canopy of Sherwood Forest, the fields, Winslow Abbey, and even the tavern — all from a dragon's point of view. I saw the gurgling stream we used to play in as kids and then a scarred battlefield in some foreign place.

The thing was, those images didn't stem from me. They were Daniel's memories, rushing from his mind to mine.

I couldn't move. I could barely breathe. Because among them, I saw myself the way Daniel saw me. Which was regular old me made much, much better. Tall and beautiful — impossibly so. Cunning and capable. Determined. Funny. Honest. All the things I wanted to be but fell short of.

The fire burst from my lungs into my veins, then rushed through the chambers of my heart and rejoined in a rush of sparks. The fire swept to the tips of my fingers and toes, filling me with heat.

Ah, the magic of a dragon kiss.

As a fox, I couldn't match that trick of his. But I could throw my own images into the mix. Like a view of Daniel above me, all that muscle glistening with a hint of sweat. His eyes, blazing like an autumn sunset. I showed him the same landscape, only from my perspective, with branches interlocking overhead. Between those were snippets of blue sky, where — *zoom!* — a dragon glided overhead.

Could Daniel sense the way that made my heart pound? Did he understand how he filled my life with love and hope, even when I was alone?

You're the one who gives me hope, he whispered into my mind.

I wanted to reply, but he came up for breath then, ending the kiss. At the same time, he unleashed a final thrust, burying himself deep.

I cried out, shuddering as we both came. Panting. Clutching each other. Gazing at a blur without registering anything but the inferno inside.

I will love you forever, Daniel's dragon roared in my mind. *I will protect. I will honor. I will respect.*

My fox panted its own vows. *I will love. Protect. Honor. I will be yours and no one else's, to forever and beyond.*

Gradually, our muscles relaxed, and we went limp. The blur took more shape, and I recalled where we were — in the tavern, not floating in our own private world. Still, I hung on to that feeling, refusing to let go. It was still the wee hours of morning. We had time.

Daniel lay over me, pressing me down in the best possible way. A long, quiet time later, he raised his head. "So, was that enough evidence to make a judgment, m'lady?"

I broke out laughing, making his body wobble over mine.

"Enough to admit you are the attraction here and not the mattress." I patted his rear. "But I do appreciate having a bed and sheets. Call it the icing on the cake."

He grinned. "Am I the cake, then?"

I nodded. "My favorite flavor."

His eyes glittered at that, inspiring all kinds of naughty ideas. "We definitely need to test that next."

Chapter Thirteen

ROBYNNE

For the past few months, I'd slept in fox form, which guaranteed a certain degree of comfort. My fur gave me a built-in blanket, and curling up gave me something — if not someone — to cuddle with. Namely, my tail. My heightened canine senses kept me alert to potential danger, even when I was asleep, and hiding away in my cozy burrow gave me a time-out from the world.

All that meant that waking up in fox form tended to be a long, lazy process.

It also meant waking up alone.

On this particular morning, however, I had the best of both worlds. I hadn't luxuriated in as slow or as lazy a morning as that one with Daniel in a long, long time. We'd made love more times than I could count, and my body was still generating heat. I was purring like a kitten, but who could blame me? With Daniel's chest for a pillow and his body to cuddle against — not to mention the aftereffects of that dragon kiss — I was in heaven.

I stretched one leg, then the other, letting my toes venture out from under the blanket. I pulled them back in just as quickly, wishing the morning could last a week. A month. A year... please?

"Good morning," Daniel whispered, tickling my ear with his lips.

I snuggled closer. "Not just good. The best. Warm blanket..." I patted the cover, then his chest. "Good pillow..."

His laugh carried through the room to the lightly frosted windowpane. "So, you're saying this is all about the bed?"

I smiled and burrowed closer to his side. "I love the bed. But the company doesn't hurt either."

"The company is the best." His arms tightened around me, and in the long, ensuing silence, my mind replayed all the melancholy nights I'd spent alone. Daniel must have done the same, because he sighed and kissed the top of my head.

"A very good morning," he whispered.

We held each other a good while longer, delaying the inevitable for as long as we could.

"Now, if only I had someone to bring me a hot drink..." I joked.

Daniel chuckled. "Getting spoiled?"

I turned in his arms. "You're the spoiled one, Sheriff. For all I know, you have three pretty girls tending to your every desire."

He snorted. "I sent them away and kept Fitzgibbon, the surliest man alive. Maybe I should recall the girls?"

I gave him a killer look. "Better not, mister. I might be tempted to aim an arrow your way."

He stuck up his hands. "I swear, I wouldn't."

I grinned. "I swear, too. And if I'm ever forced to shoot you, dear Sheriff, I'll be sure to make it look good. Right here." I swiped a finger past his right ear. "Just make sure you duck in the right direction."

"I'll make a note of that." He grinned.

We settled back in for another few minutes, content to hold each other and laze. Roosters had been crowing outside for hours, but now bleating sheep joined in. The rain had stopped, and when the earliest tavern guest departed through the door below our window, his feet slapped against mud, and he cursed.

"Another reason not to rush things," I whispered, imprinting every cozy detail into my memory.

Years ago, I'd taken such mornings for granted, but I was older and wiser now. Good times came and went like... like visitors in a tavern at the edge of the woods, I decided as the door a story below creaked open then shut.

I closed my eyes, feeling awfully civilized for an outlaw from the forest.

Outlaw... Forest... My ears perked. Was that an echo of my thoughts, or had someone outside uttered those very words?

I sat up, clutching the blanket against the morning chill.

Daniel looked up quizzically, but I focused on the voices drifting up from below. Some excitable soul had just galloped up to the door of the inn and was jabbering loudly.

"They've got him! They've got the outlaw from the forest!" the messenger said while his mount stomped restlessly in place.

Jingle, jingle. Slop, slop. I could hear the shake of the horse's bridle and the suck of the mud around its hooves.

"Robin Hood! They've got Robin Hood!" someone else took up the cry.

I skipped to the window on bare feet, eased it open, then rushed back to bed. Daniel held up the blanket, letting me dive back into the warmth.

For an instant, I was swept into the past when, after nights out exploring and making love, we would both shift to animal form to sleep under the stars. Daniel would settle in first, then lift a wing to let me curl up by his side. I would snuggle in close, listening to his heart beat, and marvel at the differences — and similarities — between Daniel the man and Daniel the dragon.

His lifting the blanket was so like lifting his wing that I was transported to easier, simpler days. But when the people outside spoke again, we huddled together, listening.

"Bugger it all. They've got Robin Hood," someone lamented.

"Don't let the sheriff hear you say that," another man warned.

Daniel made a face. "Why do they always assume I'm a bad guy?"

I laced my fingers through his. "Because the previous sheriff was such a dick?"

He nodded grimly, then lay back, pulling me with him. I followed halfheartedly, still listening.

"Robin Hood has been caught!" a third man echoed the news.

Daniel chuckled and pulled me closer. "Yes, I have her right here."

I laughed, melting against him. He was right. What did I care if they had the wrong person?

Then my gut sank. What if they had an innocent person? Or, just as bad — someone not entirely innocent, like John Little or another of the men?

"Come now," the first man broke in. "Robin Hood is far too cunning to be caught."

I would have warmed at the compliment if my body hadn't suddenly gone cold.

I might be too cunning, but that wasn't true of those I shared the camp in Sherwood Forest with. Especially one.

I buried my face in my hands, ready to moan. *God, please. No. Not him. Not now.*

Daniel stiffened as he came to the same realization. "Robert?"

I gulped. My dear, dim brother? Was he stupid enough to be caught?

My fox sighed. *Absolutely.*

I jumped out of bed, grabbing my clothes. "I have to go. I have to find out who they have."

Daniel groaned. "It could be someone else."

It could be, but somehow, I doubted that.

Daniel reluctantly followed me out of bed. "If whoever they have is innocent, I'll establish that, and we'll release him."

I pulled on my dress and grabbed for my boots. "And if it's Robert?"

Daniel looked at me without saying a word.

I shook my head and yanked on a boot. "I could kill the fool."

Daniel sat on the bed, still pinning me with that look. "I hate to say it, but..."

"Don't," I grunted, fiddling with the lace of my bodice. Last night, Daniel had opened it with one tug. Now, it was hopelessly knotted.

But Daniel, damn him, went on. "Robert has been getting in trouble ever since he was a child. Worse, he's gotten you in trouble."

I knew what Daniel was thinking. I was already an outlaw, on my way to getting a price put on my head. Why risk everything for Robert again and again?

I locked eyes with Daniel, because deep down, he must have understood.

Loyalty.

For all that Robert exasperated me, he was my brother. And it was like my father said — we only had each other. Plus, I'd promised my father to keep an eye on Robert. In my heart, I'd promised my mother too. I couldn't let either of them down.

Tears stung my eyes as I held up a hand to halt whatever Daniel was about to say. A tense silence ensued.

"What if it's a clever trap?" Daniel asked.

"Then I'll have to be cleverer."

Daniel studied me a moment longer, then sighed and reached for his trousers.

"Well, then. I suppose we ought to get him out of trouble. . . again. If it is him."

Rushing down the stairs and outside, I clung to that hope. Maybe it wasn't Robert.

Still, the forest called to me, and my fox yowled, ready to sprint.

We'll get to camp faster on four feet, my canine side said.

"Yes," Daniel cut in, reading my mind as we hurried down the muddy lane. "But even faster on a different set of four feet."

My step hitched when I caught on. "Charger?"

Daniel nodded. "You don't think I walked all the way from Nottingham — or flew?"

Of course he hadn't. He'd left Charger grazing in a dew-filled, riverside meadow. One quick whistle brought the steed running. Charger whinnied in glee, slowed the last few steps, and I swear, the two of them would have fallen into a hug if one hadn't been a horse and the other a man.

Charger nuzzled Daniel's shoulder, while Daniel scratched his cheek. And for the briefest of moments, the world was at peace. An ordinary kind of peace with chirping birds, a gurgling brook, and the whisper of wind through the trees. The kind of peace that must come as a wonder to a battle-scarred knight and his war-horse.

I stood quietly, glad they'd had each other in tough times — and unspeakably grateful they had both made it home safe.

Safe... The thought made my mind jump to Robert, and my jaw clenched.

"Time to go, Charger," Daniel murmured, snapping into action again.

He saddled the huge horse and mounted with an easy leap. Then he grinned and stuck out a hand.

"Just like old times?"

I sighed. "Only in some ways."

As a child, I'd had my run of the armory, while Daniel had free access to the stables where his father worked. We'd loved playing knight, sometimes on foot with sticks for swords, other times on horseback.

Just like old times, my fox hummed as I vaulted into the saddle behind him.

Charger took off, eager for action. But despite the thrill of riding a powerful horse at top speed — and being so close to Daniel — I mourned too, because every step brought us closer to parting.

All too quickly, Charger's hoofbeats went from thundering over hard road to muted clomps across the fields and then a cautious trot toward the riverbank. As we approached the edge of the forest, my throat went dry with fear. Had my brother truly been caught?

When Daniel halted Charger at a shallow river ford, the mighty steed pawed the ground as if he worried about Robert too. I patted his flanks, now steaming in the morning chill. Then I slid off, intent on hurrying home to find out.

But regret hit me immediately, and I looked up at my brave knight. Er — at Daniel, the sheriff. And up and up, because

Charger was that big, and Daniel all the more so atop his trusty steed.

When Daniel cocked his head in a question, I pursed my lips, then touched his leg.

"Missed my chance for a goodbye kiss."

Daniel's eyes sparkled. "Well, then. You owe me one."

I stuck a finger at him. "No, you owe me."

We both grinned, but that faded as I stepped back and turned, determined to leave quickly.

"Robynne..."

I turned back, because Daniel's voice had a new edge.

"If it is Robert... There's only so far I can bend the law, even as sheriff. And sometimes, I can't bend it at all. Often, I have no choice."

My throat went dry, but I nodded slowly.

"Neither do I," I whispered. After all, Robert was my brother.

I took another step back, then turned to go, for real this time. I splashed across the river, then glanced back.

Charger was still there, pawing the ground. Daniel's eyes met mine, and he forced a smile. The quick wave I sent him also helped me unobtrusively wipe a tear from my cheek. Then I headed into the forest, shifted, and sprinted for camp.

∞∞∞∞

I'd cursed my brother dozens of times in my life, but never so vehemently as over the hour it took to rush back to camp. I raced around the final few turns, shifted to human form, dressed quickly, and ran to our meeting place under Major Oak. Most of the men were already gathered there — not one of them merry. Even the dogs limited their usual, boisterous greeting, wagging their tails meekly.

I gulped for air. "Rumor says Robin Hood has been captured. I don't know whether to hope they've arrested an innocent man or..."

I trailed off as John Little shook his head. "Not so innocent. It's Robert."

It was one thing to guess at bad news and another to have it confirmed. When tears gnawed at my eyes, I channeled anger instead.

"Dammit, I could kill him! What fool's venture was he off on this time?"

The men studied the ground, and John chose his words carefully.

"Not so foolish this time. When you didn't come back last night..."

My gut fell. God, no. It couldn't be my fault. Please.

My mouth opened and closed, unable to produce a clear message. "But...but..."

All the shifters of Sherwood Forest came and went, including me. We all indulged the instincts that drove us to run, climb, or fly. As a bear shifter, John rambled the woods. Alan a'Dale, an eagle, loved to skim over the crowns of the trees. The others — wolves, wolverines, owls, and so on — all undertook their own forays in animal form.

But we never keep tabs on each other, I wanted to protest.

Except we did, I realized. Not directly, the way townsfolk did by counting who entered or exited the city gates, but by feel. I could always sense my fellow shifters around — or sense their absence when they strayed afield. That sense was especially keen when it came to my brother. But last night...

I buried my face in my hands. Last night, I'd been too self-absorbed to devote even the tiniest corner of my mind to Robert. But he hadn't forgotten me. If he'd sensed I was far away and unresponsive to his mental connection...

"We told him not to go, but he insisted on checking on you," John went on.

Alan took over from there. "He was following the riverside path when a patrol caught him."

Sausage, the smallest of the camp dogs, stood on his stubby back legs and snuffled at my hand, trying to offer some comfort. I leaned over to pet him, hiding my despair. Then I took a deep breath and raised my head. I couldn't let the men see me falter. But, God. How could I protect Robert now?

"Word is, a two-minute 'trial' was held," John said. "He was declared guilty of petty theft and armed robbery. The sheriff is already preparing the gallows."

I scowled. The sheriff had also been too... er, busy... to do any such thing. Even if he'd returned to Nottingham before I'd reached home, Daniel's first action would be to investigate, not to condemn.

"I flew over and saw for myself," Alan reported.

My frown deepened, and for a split second, my faith in Daniel faltered. Then I caught myself, because Daniel deserved better. But if he hadn't condemned Robert, who had?

A moment later, the answer hit me, and I all but spat the name.

"Lord Ramage."

Ramage, a man with enough spite — and authority — to condemn a man to death, especially if it polished his ego.

John narrowed his eyes. *Lord who?*

Sausage growled under his breath as if he hated the man as much as I did.

I took a deep breath, then found a stick and started sketching in the dirt. I needed a plan, and fast. A foolproof plan that couldn't count on assistance from Daniel.

"Back, silly," I muttered to Connie, the mastiff. Then I handed Alan the stick and ordered, "Show me what you saw."

The dogs watched intently as he added a few lines, then pointed to various areas. "The gallows are here. They erected a low fence here to keep spectators back..."

My stomach tightened. My brother's death, a spectacle for the masses?

My fox side growled. *Over my dead body.*

"He's locked up here, and the fountain is here..." Alan continued. "I saw them draping a red cloth over a balcony, here, for guests of honor..."

I pictured a vindictive Ramage and a conflicted Daniel. And this time, I couldn't curse Robert, only myself. I should have put an end to the thievery weeks ago. I should never have been so selfish as to spend a passionate night with my lover without thinking of the others. I should have—

I cut the thought off there. It was my fault that Robert had been captured. Therefore, it was my duty to save him. And that meant action, not regret.

I leaned over the sketch of town, thinking.

"You have a plan?" Martin asked as the others looked on eagerly.

Lord, was their faith in me humbling. I feared letting them down — especially Robert.

When I tossed the stick aside, the dogs followed in a frenzy. The men, on the other hand, pressed in hopefully — all except John, who remained doubtful. As he should be, because my only plan was to think fast.

"I do," I bluffed. "But I need time to refine it."

John raised his heavy eyebrows but didn't so much as mumble.

I needed space to think, and I needed to keep the men busy before they charged off on a foolhardy rescue mission.

"You, you, and you." I waved my arms. "Muster all our weapons. And you three — get started making more arrows. Good, straight ones. Better one sure shot than a dozen gone astray."

I could picture Robert laughing. *Lord, you sound just like Father.*

My gut tightened even more. How could I ever admit to my father that I was responsible for Robert's death?

I couldn't, so I went back to barking orders.

"You three — spears. Alan, head out for another flyover, then report back."

I barked orders until all the men scattered, intent on their missions. All but John, who stood beside me, absently rubbing his deeply scarred hand.

"Do you really have a plan?" he murmured.

"Not yet, but I will."

You'd better, my fox muttered.

I scowled and went back to thinking. All morning and for most of the afternoon, when I finally called the men in for a meeting.

"All right. This is the plan," I announced, making sure I sounded supremely confident, even if I wasn't. "Listen closely..."

Chapter Fourteen

DANIEL

The criminal was indeed Robert, as a glance through the peep-hole in the dungeon door confirmed. I'd already picked up on his wolf scent — barely, though, given the stench of the dungeon — so a glance was all I needed. I quickly retreated before Robert could spot me.

Oh, Daniel! Great to see you! I pictured the fool announcing. *Did Robynne send you?*

It would be hard enough for me to save him when no one suspected me. If anyone discovered we'd grown up together, it would be even harder — and nigh impossible with Lord Ramage breathing over my shoulder from the moment I raced back into town.

"A wonderful day for Nottingham, don't you agree?" Ramage practically sang as he struggled to keep up with my long steps.

I paced outside wordlessly. The sun was blinding after the dim dungeons, but I charged ahead. I had to figure out what to do — and more importantly, to guess what Robynne had planned. That she would sweep in to rescue her brother was a given. The question was how, and how much help did she need from me?

I frowned. How much help was I able to offer?

And there it was, the same old conundrum. Helping Robynne meant helping the locals, but if my support was discovered, I would be the one to hang. Nottingham would be assigned a new sheriff who would take a harsh stance — not just on bandits like Robynne, but on locals who benefited from her work.

"Yes, it's a wonderful day in Nottinghaaa—" Ramage's gleeful words ended with a yelp as he slipped.

The previous night's rain had left an inch of mud oozing over most of the city. Too bad Ramage caught himself before wallowing like a pig.

I paused midway across the parade grounds, scowling. There, at Nottingham's highest point, the castle keep stood to my left and town hall on my right. Between them stood some of the finest houses in town, all built in the modern, half-timbered style. Unlike the market square down by the city gates, this space was dotted with flagpoles for special occasions.

Like today. It was ridiculous, the number of banners flying in celebration.

"Take those down immediately," I ordered the soldier at the head of the misplaced initiative.

"But, sir, we haven't had a good hanging in months!"

I shouldn't have been surprised that it was Grove — the same soldier who'd manhandled that innocent boy weeks before — the boy who'd found the first coin Robynne left in the fountain. Somehow, Grove's energy had to be channeled into less destructive purposes. I made a mental note to place him in charge of decorating at Christmas.

If you're still in the job by then, my dragon reminded me.

"Take them down," I barked.

Grove looked around mournfully. "Even the yellow ones?"

"All of them! Now!" I bellowed.

The men hammering at the base of the gallows flinched, and the citizens who'd been watching scattered. Two stopped to eye me from a distance.

You know, I was starting to think he wasn't too bad as far as sheriffs go, I imagined one whispering the other. *But I'm starting to have my doubts.*

I'll never forgive the man who hangs Robin Hood, I was sure the surly one muttered in reply. *Never.*

Meanwhile, I bet the soldiers were complaining bitterly. *The previous sheriff let us hang banners...*

Lord, I hated my job.

It would be so much easier to join Robynne in the forest, my dragon agreed. *To be a hero instead of... of...*

I sighed. Instead of being the guy trying to minimize consequences for average citizens. How heroic was that?

Then again, the Crusades had taught me that the greatest heroes were usually unsung. Generals who retreated rather than sending soldiers to senseless deaths. Simple farmers doing their best to feed their families. Mothers stretched to their limits yet refusing to give up for their children's sake.

All those people must have felt their backs to the wall, as I now did. Yet they found solutions, no matter how desperate. I had to do the same.

But what?

I couldn't grant Robert a reprieve. Lord Ramage was determined to punish the culprit — any culprit. Worse, he had the power to do so. As sheriff, I held the highest commoner's rank in town, but all it took was one nobleman with connections to the crown and my hands were tied as surely as Robert's were shackled.

Even if it weren't Ramage causing a fuss now, some other nobleman would come along sooner or later to demand the same measures. The more the legend of Robin Hood grew, the more determined authorities would be to show decisive action. And what was more decisive than a hanging?

I closed my eyes, imagining a noose tightening around my own neck.

My breath grew heated with my dragon's anger. *Why did that fool have to let himself get captured now of all times?*

A fresh breeze ghosted in from the north, and I was sure I heard a whisper. *Destiny.*

I kicked the ground. Whose destiny? Robert's? Mine? Robynne's? Or was it all just a cruel game?

I pondered that while pacing and trying to think of a solution. By late afternoon, I'd only succeeded in the pacing part. All too soon, the sun cast long, solemn shadows over

Nottingham. The hammering on the main square ceased, and the gallows silently awaited their prize. Townsfolk lined the streets, equally quiet and grim.

"Hang Robin Hood and you might as well hang us all," one man muttered, though I pretended not to hear.

Then the dungeon doors ground open, and wagon wheels creaked. A ripple went through the crowd. It was time to parade Robert through town on his way to an ugly end.

The wagon was old and unadorned, much like the horse pulling it and the man guiding both. Old. Emotionless. Cold.

Clip, clop. Clip, clop. Hoofbeats echoed through the eerily silent town.

Hundreds of people crowded the street, staring. And it truly was a sight to behold. A noble bandit, standing casually while the wagon rattled along.

My dragon chuckled without any humor. *Ah, Robert. He always had a bit of an actor in him.*

Tight-lipped men looked on, their hands balled into fists, powerless to stop their hero's death. Teary-eyed women tossed flowers as the wagon rolled past.

"Bless you, Robin Hood," one after another murmured.

I glanced around. Robynne had no doubt concealed herself among the people, along with the Merry Men. Did her heart swell a little, knowing she was the one who'd earned that respect?

My dragon snorted. *More likely, Robynne is coolly fingering an arrow tip, ready to launch her rescue plan.*

I prayed it would be enough, whatever it was. Robynne was as cunning as a fox — literally — but even she would be hard-pressed to succeed. Every soldier in the shire had been called up to duty, and their numbers were augmented by Ramage's private guards. Usually, hangings took place outside the city walls, but Robert's would be in the very heart of Nottingham, where escape would be harder. Lord Ramage had insisted on that.

The man was human, but I could see the monster in his eyes. A being who delighted in the suffering of others.

He's the one who should be hanged, my dragon growled.

The sentiment came with a whiff of smoke that burned my nose. I fought it back reluctantly, yearning to finally reveal myself. How gratifying that would be! To raise my arms, let them stretch into wings, then flash my long fangs. To spit fire and watch Ramage grovel for his life. I could free Robert's bonds with one quick claw swipe, then soar off to some forgotten corner of the kingdom to live happily ever after with the woman I loved.

For the next few heartbeats, my imagination pursued those tantalizing thoughts. Wouldn't Robynne love me even more for saving her brother? Oh, and maybe I didn't even have to leave. As a dragon, I could command Nottingham any way I saw fit. Everyone, from humble farmer to haughty soldier, would have to bow to my will. Robynne and I could live in the castle at the highest point of town, and no one would dare object to any of our whims.

My pulse quickened, and my chest swelled.

But a moment later, I cringed. Lord, no. I didn't want any of those things. Those fantasies were a delusion — the kind I'd seen ruthless overlords pursue in vain. Ultimately, they lost everything — especially the most precious commodity of all.

Respect.

The word echoed in my ears as I walked uphill, part of the silent procession toward death.

Respect. At that moment, Robert commanded it. And even if most of it was misplaced, he did genuinely cut a dashing figure. Despite having his hands bound behind his back, he stood tall and proud as the wagon lurched along, eyes unwaveringly, unrepentantly ahead.

Yes, Robert truly had manned up to the occasion. But that wouldn't save him.

As a dragon, I could, but it wasn't worth it — not to myself, nor the people of Nottingham in the long-term. The trade-off was only worth it to Robynne, who loved her brother unconditionally.

All right, then, my dragon declared. *We'll leave it to Robynne to save her dimwit brother. All we have to do is buy her time to enact her plan.*

My lips formed a tight line. Her plan was bound to be both brilliant and insane.

Worst case? Everything would go terribly wrong—

— *as it's bound to,* my dragon grumbled, *since Robert is involved.*

— and Robert would be hanged. Robynne would try to intervene but be captured. I would shift to save her, but if I were a moment too late, she would be killed. Then...

My dragon cut off those thoughts. *Focus. We need to buy Robynne time.*

The procession grew as I followed the wagon along the high street toward the main square. At the next intersection, drummers took up the rear with a relentless, solemn beat. Grove's idea, no doubt.

Ramage ate it up. I gnashed my teeth. Rows of grim spectators looked on, then filled in behind us after we passed. The whole damn spectacle was turning into the event of the decade — one people would immortalize in stories they passed on for generations, like the great fire of 1029 or the mighty storm of 1172.

It made me sick. Robert didn't deserve the adulation. Robynne did.

Where is she, dammit? my dragon grumbled, scanning the crowd.

Several times, a face, voice, or just a shadow made me do a double take. But by the time I looked more closely, she was gone, if she had ever been there at all.

My eye caught on a few men in the crowd, too — in hoods, hats, or heavy cloaks. I could smell shifters on the prowl — a wolf here, a bear there — but I couldn't pick them out from the dense crowd.

Ramage leaned in to chuckle. "Let the townsfolk learn their lesson today. That I am not a man to be trifled with, and that crime doesn't pay."

My disdain must have shown, because Ramage leaned in ever closer, dropping his voice in warning. "Much like neglect of duty — another crime punishable by death."

Was he onto me? No surprise, I supposed. I'd spent an hour that morning trying to reduce Robert's sentence. I'd pointed out that Ramage's wagon train hadn't been held up in Sherwood Forest, and that there was no evidence of Robert's crimes, only hearsay. I'd also demanded a fair trial by a judge and council of peers, but Ramage had just scoffed.

I'm all the judge you need, and if I say he's guilty, he's guilty.

I nearly bared my dragon teeth. They pressed on my gums, intent on release.

I glared at Ramage, tempted to say, *Great leaders lead by great deeds, not by oppression.*

Six trumpets blared as we entered the main square, where another hundred people waited. Other townsfolk pressed in from behind until no more would fit — and even then, more squeezed in.

Overhead, an eagle circled. I squinted. The same eagle I'd seen before?

I nearly paused to study it, but Ramage cut left for the castle and its balcony. As distant kin of Nottingham's absent lord, that was his prerogative. I hesitated, then followed. Much as it turned my stomach to join him, the balcony offered the best place to look for Robynne — and a handy place to take off from in dragon form.

A last-ditch effort I hoped to avoid. But, Lord. I was starting to sweat.

Outside, hundreds of angry eyes had sliced into me. In the cool, echoing halls of the castle, suits of armor stood stiffly along the walls, scrutinizing me with ghostly gazes. When I stepped out onto the balcony, the sun hit me again, along with the sound of the crowd. A bitter murmur sounded as citizens looked between Robert and me with expressions that demanded, *Well? Aren't you going to do something?*

My face was expressionless, but inside, I warred with myself. Was I? Wasn't I?

Chapter Fifteen

DANIEL

One. Two. Three. Rough wooden stairs creaked as Robert was led to the gallows. The platform was high enough to ensure everyone a clear view. The rope, however, was short — short enough to ensure Robert a slow, tortured death. It was all too easy to imagine the horrible choking noises he would make and the way his body would writhe in a macabre dance until it went limp.

Bile rose to my throat. Death was part of life. That wasn't the issue. But painful, premature deaths... those, not even the hardest veteran of war got used to.

Even the executioner — Paul, the butcher — looked like he was having second thoughts.

I never liked him, my dragon sniffed.

Ramage, on the other hand, looked positively gleeful. No doubt he'd paid off Paul in a deal the latter already regretted. The locals were sure to run him out of town by sunset.

I pursed my lips. They would do the same with me. Dammit! In the short time Ramage had been in town, he'd undone weeks of toiling to earn a little respect.

"Bless you, Robin Hood!" An older woman made the sign of the cross.

"We love you, Robin!" Young women wept and blew kisses.

Robert winked back, totally unperturbed. Was he supremely confident his sister would rescue him? Unafraid of death? Just plain stupid?

My dragon sighed. *All of the above.*

Giles, the captain of the guard, unscrolled an official-looking document and announced, "On this day of our Lord 1193, by order of the Great Lord Ramage..."

A low hiss emerged from the crowd, and the eyes that turned toward the balcony shot daggers. Still, Giles droned on.

"...and in the name of God, and the King of England, and our good Prince John..."

More hisses sounded. Ramage signaled his man, who nudged Giles to move things along.

"...et cetera, et cetera." Giles made a churning motion and skipped ahead. "You, Robin Hood, are hereby pronounced guilty of banditry, to be executed from life into death. May God have mercy on your soul." Giles finished and turned to Robert. "This is your opportunity, sir, to pray for mercy."

Robert opened his mouth, and the crowd hushed.

"Great Lord who?" he deadpanned, making everyone hoot.

Ramage clutched the railing of the balcony, his face bright red. He leaned forward, scowling at Giles, who shoved Robert onto a small stool.

Ramage snorted. "Nottingham is so behind the times. A trapdoor does the job with so much more flair."

Flair? Is this a hanging or a dance competition? my dragon grumbled.

My fingernails ached as my beast clawed closer to the surface. Meanwhile, Giles beckoned a priest up to the platform for a final prayer.

I looked away, determined to find Robynne. I started from the back of the crowd this time, where a man held his daughter high and whispered. Was he praising the bandit's bravery or teaching her that crime didn't pay?

I continued my search of the crowd, but instinct pulled me back to the priest. Something was out of place there. Maybe not the brown robe, the deep hood concealing his face, or the cross hanging from his neck, but something else...

Maybe it was his build, because this was definitely not a man who spent his days contemplating the Bible. He had the body of a warrior, with broad, muscled shoulders that loose robe couldn't hide. A man I would have liked to have fighting by my side in the toughest, most brutal battles.

The priest whispered to the condemned man, then, moving with catlike grace and precision, he took up position at the very edge of the platform.

I frowned. Taking up position to do what, exactly?

To do more than take a criminal's confession, my dragon hummed in approval.

Then it hit me. That was the friar from the abbey, and he was on Robynne's side. I glanced around. Who else?

My eyes roved the crowd, studying one solemn face after another. If Robynne's men were any good, they would blend in, tricking an observer to skip over them. Which I nearly did, until a sixth sense had me back up to observe a boy over on the left.

Not a boy, my dragon chuckled.

I looked closer. Robynne?

One moment, she was there, and the next, she had disappeared like a fox in a thicket. Moments later, I glimpsed the tip of a wooden stick — a bow? — and a slight, youthful figure moving through the crowd. Was that Robynne?

Normally, I could feel her presence. But with the crowd, Robert's looming death sentence, and a mind still spinning for a way out of this mess, I couldn't home in on Robynne as usual.

Maybe she wasn't even there. Ramage had doubled the guard at each of the city gates, and it would have taken a miracle for Robynne and her men to slip through — with or without weapons.

My dragon lashed its tail. *So let me be the weapon.*

The drummers started up again. The executioner looped the noose around Robert's neck. He gulped, and I did the same.

My fingers twitched, clawing the air.

Let me out, my dragon growled. *We'll free Robert. Kill Ramage. We'll show them all what we're capable of and live far away from this miserable place.*

The man in the back of the crowd lifted his daughter off his shoulders and turned away. A stark reminder that the people of Nottingham needed a sheriff like me, not the tyrant who would be sure to replace me if I exposed myself now.

My throat burned. *Never mind that. We can join Robynne in the forest.*

I wanted to believe it, but I knew we were most effective in our current constellation: Robynne pushing the limits on one side of the law, and me pulling on the other.

Doomed, in other words, to deny our love forever?

Beside me, Ramage scowled. "Do it, already," he grunted, as if the executioner could hear. "Kill him. Show them all."

Let me show them all and kill Ramage, my dragon growled.

The executioner braced his legs and started pulling the rope tight. It ran up and over the arm of the gallows, then down to Robert's neck. *Cr-cr-cr-creak.* Wood and rope groaned while Robert stretched to his toes in a hopeless bid for survival. Still, the executioner pulled, making Robert tilt sideways and go up on one toe. All it would take now was one push, and Robert would be swinging.

I gritted my teeth. Still no Robynne in sight. No rescue crew. No way out of this impossible situation.

Dammit, I wanted to yell at the friar. At the crowd. At fate. *Do something!*

But no one did anything. Except the executioner, who kicked the stool out from under Robert, leaving him dangling.

"No!" a dozen people in the crowd cried.

No! my soul echoed.

"I give him thirty seconds, maximum," one of the soldiers behind me murmured.

If only Robynne were there with a well-placed arrow. But even if she was, it was an impossible shot, given the narrow rope and the way it swung with Robert's desperate movements. The most Robynne could hope to accomplish was a mercy shot at her brother's heart.

Robert jerked his elbows and feet desperately. But with his arms tied behind his back, it was hopeless.

As hopeless as my love for Robynne?

My dragon roared inside, and just like that, my decision was made.

I was tired of hopeless. Tired of misery. Tired of letting destiny play cruel games.

Sucking in air to feed the fire within me, I lifted my arms in a wide, sweeping motion, preparing to shift. Every muscle tensed as my shoulders pulled back, morphing into wings. The fabric of the back of my shirt split, and Ramage looked over, confused.

Enjoy the last few beats of your heart, my dragon snickered.

I couldn't wait to see his eyes grow wide in horror as his plans unraveled. But something whizzed through my peripheral vision, and we both whipped around to follow it.

Thwack!

It all happened in an instant. The blur of an arrow, cutting through the air. The sound of it slicing through the hangman's rope, then spiking into the frame of the gallows. The thump of Robert's feet as he dropped back to the platform, gasping.

A dozen voices broke out at the same time, and everyone milled around in confusion.

"What?"

"How?"

"Wait!"

The soldiers around me gaped while Ramage pointed toward Robert. "No! Stop! Get him!"

Halting my shift quickly, I watched, not quite believing. But, yes. An arrow really had parted the rope, and Robert was no longer hanging. He was on all fours, gulping for air. The muscular friar hauled Robert to his feet and hustled him down the stairs, away from the gallows.

Someone in the crowd cheered, and the outcry went from confusion to celebration.

"Did you see that shot? One in a million!"

Just what my muddled mind was thinking. Like Ramage and so many others, I turned in the direction the arrow had come from.

And there she was — Robynne, perched on a barrel, her bow still quivering.

I grinned, soaking in the sight. Her hood was up, concealing her face, but there was no mistaking that no-nonsense stance and lithe figure.

My mate, my dragon hummed proudly. *One in a million.*

What took you so long? I couldn't help but joke.

Her lips quirked. *Just checking.*

I frowned, slow to understand — until it clicked. Had she waited to see if I was willing to risk everything for her brother?

Anger welled up in me but faded in the next instant. If I were the bandit and she were the sheriff, could I have resisted one last chance to put my suspicions to rest forever?

Not for your brother, I corrected. *For you, my love.*

Time stood still, and our bond erased the distance between us. My cheeks warmed, and my soul danced. For that instant, nothing seemed to separate us, and nothing ever would.

Then time snapped back into motion, and Ramage shouted, "Get him! Get that archer!"

Robynne yanked out another arrow and aimed at us.

Then, yikes — the arrow was already flying, and the words she'd laughed in the tavern echoed in my mind.

If I'm ever forced to shoot you, I'll make sure to make it look good. Just make sure you duck in the right direction.

And whoa! I did, but barely.

Zoom! The arrow whizzed past my ear, then smacked against the stone wall of the castle.

The guards around me yelped, taking cover.

I shot Robynne a look. She grinned and drew another arrow.

"Get him! Get him!" Ramage pointed.

I could see Robynne's lips move as she silently corrected him. *Her, you moron. Get her.*

"Watch out!" someone yelled.

Ramage's eyes went wide as he realized he was the bull's-eye. He gaped, frozen in place, as if such a notion were impossible. *No one shoots at me, the mighty Lord Ramage.*

But they did — or, at least, one did. Robynne.

Ramage tried to duck, but I grabbed his arm, keeping him upright.

"What are you doing?" he protested.

Making sure the shot lands where it belongs, my dragon growled.

And, *clunk!* The arrow made a strangely muted sound as it buried itself in Ramage's chest, thrusting him back.

He hit a wall and gasped, clutching the protruding arrow. His eyes met mine, and I could see the exact moment he put it all together.

Yes, that archer is Robynne — the Robin you thought you'd captured, but you didn't. The woman you planned to marry for all the wrong reasons. And, yes. I'm on her side. My eyes heated as I glared the message into him. *Now, you're finally getting what you deserve. Death. Can you see it coming?*

Fear seeped into his eyes like the blood oozing through his tunic.

"But...you...him..."

Her, my dragon bellowed. *Robynne is a her! Will you finally give her credit?*

"Lord Ramage!" one of the guards sputtered from where he'd taken cover.

Ramage turned to him, mumbling. A last effort to spring my cover, no doubt.

"Oh dear. Not Lord Ramage." I drowned out his protests and leaned over, almost as if to comfort him in his last moments.

Almost.

"Goodbye and good riddance," I snarled, though I kept it quiet. "From Robynne."

Ramage stared as he finally made the connection. Then his eyes went distant, fixing on a point behind me forever.

I let him drop as the guards huddled around, chattering. "Lord Ramage, dead!"

"You were nearly hit too, sir," one told me.

"Lucky miss," someone else marveled.

Ha. If only they knew.

I gestured over the square, where pandemonium had broken out. "Quick! We must keep them from escaping!"

I said *quick*, but I made sure Ramage's body fell between us, gaining me precious seconds to observe the scene below.

Robynne had jumped down from the barrel and was racing around the outer edge of the square, where the crowds were thinner. Meanwhile, the friar had cut Robert's bonds and was hustling him to safety. A circle of men pressed in around them, forming a barrier to the few guards who dared intervene. Overhead, an eagle circled, its piercing cries heralding victory.

Not too soon, I wanted to warn them. The city gates were all manned, and Robynne couldn't lead her entire band through the secret passage behind the bakery.

To the west gate, I called into her mind, hoping she would catch the message amid the pandemonium. *There are just as many guards there, but I made sure to assign the laziest men to a single location.*

I couldn't see her, but I could hear the smile in her voice. *You, my mate, are a genius.*

I sighed. No, she was the genius. I just did my best to keep up. Somehow.

And off she went, leading her men down a side street.

"Robin Hood! Robin Hood!" Townsfolk raised their arms in jubilation.

"They're heading to the south gate!" I said as the guards on the balcony stumbled closer.

Luckily, they didn't question how I knew that. They just echoed the words.

"To the south gate!" their shouts boomed across the square. "Hurry!"

"No, wait!" I bellowed out, making the captain of the guard look up with an expression that asked, *Why wait now?*

I couldn't exactly say, *Because I want to give Robynne as much of a head start as possible,* so I settled for, "They're armed, dangerous, and desperate. I want you and your men in tight formation before you follow. Wait until I'm there to lead you. I don't want another life lost to those bandits."

One of the men beside me eyed the body. "Poor Lord Ramage."

Inwardly, I snorted. He got what he deserved.

"You stay here. Guard the body," I ordered. Ramage didn't deserve special treatment, but the fewer men free to chase Robynne, the better. Then I took off, racing through the castle to join Giles at the edge of the square.

"I came as fast as I could," I assured him.

Well, sort of, my dragon chuckled.

I waved the guards forward. Losing precious time to maintain tight formation, we advanced down the street.

"They could be anywhere..." I warned.

The men crept along at a snail's pace, nervously eyeing every turn and every alley. I sent the most competent to the south gate and led the rest westward, going as slowly — er, quickly — as I could. There, we found the city gates flung wide open and a dozen groaning soldiers.

"They came out of nowhere," one of the guards mumbled, rubbing his head.

"I swear, they outnumbered us, ten to one," another insisted.

I jogged past them and stopped a few steps outside the gate, grinning at the silhouettes of a dozen animals loping off into the sunset. Wolves, bears, wolverines, and yes... a fox leading the way, her copper tail held proudly.

I leaned against a wall, watching them go, exhilarated but filled with sorrow too.

It had been close, but we'd done it. I'd done it — I'd protected Robynne.

Then I slumped, closing my eyes.

"It's all right, sir," one of the men reassured me. "We'll get them next time."

That wasn't what ate at me. It was the realization that there would be a next time, and another, and another. To protect Robynne, I had to remain where I was. Achingly, painfully, agonizingly apart from my true love.

I yearned to join those carefree, footloose, fancy-free shifters who lived as they pleased. But no. I had to continue my charade. Me, Sheriff of Nottingham. Keeper of the peace, nemesis of all outlaws — especially the merry band living in Sherwood Forest.

I sighed, then squinted into the sunset.

"Good Lord," somebody exclaimed. "Is that a wolf I see?"

I snorted. What would he say if I joined them as a dragon?

I patted his shoulder. "Now then, Mr. Sattler. That knock to your head might be more serious than you thought."

He blinked a few times, then wobbled back inside. "You're right. Bloody bandits."

I turned toward the forest in time to see the fox jump onto a rock and glance back. The wind ruffled her fur, making it glint in the last rays of the sun.

We gazed at each other for a long time. Then one of the wolves yipped, making Robynne turn away. After a wistful glance back at me, she joined the rest. She had to, and we both knew it.

I would have given anything to run after her then. No, to fly after her, like that stupid eagle who seemed to follow wherever she went.

But I couldn't. All I could do was lean against the wall and watch my true love disappear into the forest.

Chapter Sixteen

ROBYNNE

That evening in Sherwood Forest, our celebration was muted. First, because we all knew what a close shave it had been. Second, because I'd nearly decked Robert for getting caught and putting us all in danger. I'd hugged him instead, but I did shake him a couple of times afterward.

Still, I had to admit Robert had done himself proud.

"You've done the family proud," I murmured when I reeled him in for a second hug.

His eyes were misty, and his voice wavered when he whispered, "You think so?"

Yes, I did. Truly.

I nodded, then poked him with a finger. "But if you ever do that again, I'll kill you."

Everyone laughed, and John smacked my back lightly.

"Come on, Robynne. I think he's learned his lesson. Let's celebrate."

And everyone did. Well, nearly everyone. I sat to one side, watching the men eat, joke, sing, and even dance around the blazing campfire.

"I swear, your neck is an inch longer," Martin teased Robert.

"And other parts an inch shorter," Alan added, making everyone roar in laughter.

Things went on in that vein for a while, with jokes and jibes washed down with copious amounts of food and ale. I didn't fuss over how much that reduced our supplies for the coming winter, because the men had earned it. We'd all earned it.

That was the satisfying part — the realization that we'd gone from a loose band of bandits to... well, a force to be reckoned with. I thought back to how intently every man had listened to my plan, and how each had followed it to the letter. Every one of them had shown discipline and restraint.

"Couldn't have done it without you," John murmured, taking a seat beside me.

I flashed a weak smile. "Not sure about that."

There was Daniel, after all. But much as I wanted to publicly credit him, I struggled to do so. It was just too awkward to come out with something like, *Don't forget the hunky sheriff — the man who screwed me senseless the night before all this happened. Good thing he's on our side, huh?*

John gestured with his ale mug, making some of the froth spill over. "We might have freed Robert on our own, but I doubt we would have made it out of town alive. At least, not all of us."

My gut tightened, because I was the one who'd set off the chain of events by spending the night with Daniel.

John shrugged. "All's well that ends well."

I glanced over at the big bear shifter. Had he read my mind?

Hard to tell, because John changed the subject. "That friar you recruited is a good man. Tuck, right?"

I nodded. I'd detoured to the monastery on my way to Nottingham earlier that day to ask for Tuck's help in our plan, and he'd agreed immediately.

"The poor man is dying for action," I explained. "Anything. He's just not cut out for the clergy."

"Why not invite him to join us?"

Tuck had asked as much himself, but I'd had to turn him down. Like Daniel, he was more valuable in his current position.

The ache in my heart never really ceased, but at that reminder, it doubled. I blew out a long breath, then stood. John did the same, towering above me.

"Heading to bed already?" he teased.

It would have been so easy to nod and pretend. But, no. Earlier, John had mentioned Robert learning his lesson. In truth, it was I who'd learned mine.

"No. I'm going to... um...." I stirred the air with a hand, trying to put it delicately.

John tilted his head, waiting. "Let your fox out for a good run?"

"Yes. No. Not exactly...." I fumbled a little longer, then forced it out. "I have to go meet someone. It's fine, I promise," I added quickly. "Someone I trust. Someone who made rescuing Robert possible."

John nodded slowly. "Someone like that sheriff, for example?"

I froze. None of the men could know my secret. No one in town either — well, except the baker and his daughter. It was too dangerous — and heck, too damn complicated to explain.

But, shoot. John knew. Damn the bear, with his quiet demeanor and sharp senses that missed nothing.

Me and the sheriff? Don't be silly, I nearly protested. But I didn't want the men to lie to me, so I couldn't lie to them. I was too tongue-tied anyway.

"I've seen him look at you, and you look at him," John whispered, careful not to let the others hear.

"I don't look at him!"

John laughed. "And when you came back after a long night out, you smelled of sex and dragon."

I'd outfoxed death in a dozen different ways in my life, but at that moment, I thought I would die of embarrassment.

John stuck up his hands nonchalantly. "Not my place to ask, and certainly not my place to tell. Besides, I trust you. We all do."

My throat went dry. From day one, I'd had to fight for the respect and trust of this band of outlaws. Now that I had it, responsibility weighed heavily on my shoulders. I couldn't let these men down. Ever.

I cleared my throat, but even then, I sounded like a cat choking on a hairball. "Thank you. I mean it." An awkward moment later, I added, "About Daniel, though — no one can know. Please. No one."

John pursed his lips, then nodded earnestly. "Right." Then he raised his voice loud enough for everyone to hear. "Off you go to bed, you lightweight."

I smiled my thanks, then whispered, "Don't let Robert assume the worst if I'm not back by morning."

John raised his mug again. "Have fun, chief. You deserve it."

I wasn't sure I did, but I did use the chance to slip away from the others.

A good man, that John Little, my fox mused when I'd shifted and trotted into the forest.

I nodded. A good man, indeed. Like the rest of the Sherwood Forest outlaws — a little rough around the edges, but all heart inside.

All heart, my fox sighed. *All honor. A lot like Daniel.*

With that, I quickened my pace.

Chapter Seventeen

ROBYNNE

I never had to ponder where to head or whether Daniel would come. I knew he would. All I had to do was get to the right place as quickly as I could. Sherwood Forest was a huge, undulating stretch of woods, with only a handful of places a dragon might land. The best was a big, rocky bluff called White Horse Crag. But anyone seeking a dragon would look there first.

Instead, I headed for Poor Knight's Castle, a dramatic rock face that sloped sharply on one side and fell off vertically on the other. The name came from the ancient structure near the peak — mere ruins now, but exactly the kind of place Daniel and I loved to explore as kids. The updraft made for tricky landings, but I was sure Daniel could do it.

It took a good hour to run there at a brisk fox pace, and a full ten minutes to pick my way through the boulder field at the base of the slope. Finally, I emerged at the top, where the great hall of the castle had once hosted huge feasts.

Three of the four walls still stood, though only to the height of an ornate doorway that was now a gaping hole in the otherwise seamless perimeter. The far wall had vanished along with a section of the cliff, so as I crossed the grassy floor of the great hall, I ran toward nothingness. Then, at the cliff's edge, I stopped and looked out.

At first, I thought I was alone, but that was because I looked straight out. Silly me.

I fluffed my tail and licked my fur, making myself presentable. Then the wind whistled, and I looked up.

Daniel, I whispered.

The sound emerged as a canine chuff, and I backed up, making space for him to land.

He'd been there for some time, I realized, circling overhead. Watching. Hoping. Waiting. For me.

Even in my teens, I'd never been the giddy or fluttery-eyed type. But in that moment, my soul lifted, my blood rushed, and yes — there might have been a little giddy fluttering. I couldn't help it.

As a man, Daniel turned heads. As a dragon... Well, it was hard to find words. Suffice to say, if he were spotted soaring over Nottingham, the whole place would grind to a halt. He was that big, that fierce. That mighty. And all that without spitting fire!

His wings were huge, leathery spans, his neck long and sleek. His tail stroked the air, initiating a turn. And his eyes... two huge, sky-blue orbs glowing down at me. Me!

He circled once more, then glided in for landing, coming straight for me. It ought to have been a terrifying moment, but I pranced in place, thrilled.

And, *whoosh!* When he scooped his wings, displaced air pressed my fur flat. Then came the *thump, thump, thump* of his first steps across the ground and the grumble of his greeting. At least, it was a grumble in dragon-speak. But the voice that sounded in my mind was soft and serene.

My love. My love...

He echoed the words over and over as he stood with his wings spread wide.

Still in fox form, I rose on my back legs, yipping in glee.

My love. I missed you so much.

Being upright made shifting natural, and I went from balancing on two paws to striding toward him on bare human feet. My heart skipped as I strode into that mighty dragon hug. A human onlooker would have screamed to me to run for my life, but I knew better. Besides, there were no witnesses, only weathered stones, tangled weeds, and the moon and stars above.

Daniel began his own shift, so that when our bodies met a moment later, it was in a human hug. If our timing hadn't been perfect, I would have smacked ingloriously against the leathery plates of his chest.

But our timing was perfect, because that was the way it was with mates.

Daniel held me, whispering, "Robynne..."

I pressed my face into the nook between his shoulder and neck. Moonlight bathed our bare shoulders as we stood, holding each other tight. Eventually, I pulled back and cupped his face. We had so much to talk about, but instinct took over, and all I could do was kiss, kiss, and kiss.

Or rather, kiss, touch, and caress. It didn't take much to get a dragon aroused — in a good way, in this case — and before long, we'd shuffled over to a flat slab of rock and settled down, intertwined.

"Not too cold?" Daniel murmured between the hungry kisses he pressed lower and lower along my center line.

I laughed. Inside, I was on fire.

"Not with a dragon to keep me warm — oh!" I ended with a squeak when Daniel touched my most sensitive place.

Those were the last coherent words I uttered for a while. The rest were happily tortured cries as he reduced me to a whimpering, moaning mess. Because, well — dragon. Even in human form, they didn't hold back.

Neither did foxes, and a few breathless minutes later, I was repaying his favor. Because we foxes, well... We had talents too.

The funny thing was, no matter how creative or out of control our lovemaking became, instinct inevitably guided us to the best position to reach a crescendo. I lay back, and Daniel came down over, then into me with one smooth, hard thrust. Then another and another, which I matched with upward bucks. Again and again, until we moved in a frenzy, and finally, we both cried out in release.

Then we went limp, back to where we'd started — holding each other tight.

Eventually, Daniel rolled aside and nestled beside me, gently combing stray strands of hair into place.

"Why is it that days — even years — pass so slowly, but a minute with you rushes by?"

I smiled, though it was bittersweet. "Because what we have is the real thing."

He pulled me closer. "Must be."

It was an echo of talks we'd had in younger days, when we felt just as deep a bond but had little to test it. But Lord, did we have plenty testing us nowadays.

"We need to think of something," I finally said. I yearned to act, to take charge of our own fates.

Daniel looked at me, waiting.

I clasped his hand. "Join me. Join us in Sherwood Forest. Lord knows I can use all the help I can get with the Merry Men." The shine in Daniel's eyes told me how tempted he was, so I ran with it. "We could live and work side by side. We could battle the bad, support the good..."

"Why don't you join *me*?" He leaned closer, speaking seductively. "Just think. You could even sleep in a bed. Every night."

I laughed. "Now, you're really tempting me."

We grinned at each other, savoring that one lighthearted moment.

"Seriously, though," Daniel continued. "Robert seems to have grown up. Why not leave the banditry to him and work with me on the inside?"

I wished I could. But I couldn't. "I know those men too well. Left to their own devices, they'll find more trouble."

A long silence ensued, and my despair grew. "Will we never get to be together?"

Daniel kissed me, then ran a finger down my cheek. "I want *us* more than anything. But what we've set in motion won't stop by itself. Word has already reached London. From what I hear, everyone is talking about Robin Hood. If this continues, Prince John will send an army and torch the forest to the ground."

For the first time that night, a chill crept into my bones. I pictured the birds that sang from the thick foliage. Dappled fawns waiting for does to return and care for them. Oaks older than living memory... All that would be threatened.

No matter how angrily I worked my jaw, the truth remained.

"So, we leave." I gestured, throwing together a plan. "We head to the borderlands and make a life there. You and me." I tapped his chest, tempted to charge off immediately.

But Daniel just looked at me, and a moment later, I slumped. "Nice fantasy, huh?"

He ran a hand over my shoulder. "I've never been more tempted, but that won't help the people here."

Damn the man for his sense of duty.

He flashed a little smile. "You always said you wanted to go crusading. Here's your chance. Right here. Maybe my chance, too."

"You've already been to the Crusades."

His eyes darkened. "But did I achieve any good? Or did I simply add to the misery?"

Unsure how to respond, I held my tongue.

"But maybe this is my chance," he went on, more upbeat. "Think about it. As sheriff, I can finally do some good. You, too. You achieve that by continuing what you're doing."

I frowned. "You don't want to be together every day and every night?"

He shook his head fiercely. "I want that. I dream about it. I live for that day. But this isn't about us, Robynne. It's about something bigger. Something better."

I bit my lip. As a child, I'd dreamed of being a brave, selfless knight. But this was no longer a child's fantasy. It was real life, and the sacrifice was more than I could bear.

Still, Daniel was right. This wasn't about us. It was about doing the right thing.

"So, we keep this up indefinitely?" I grumbled.

He shook his head. "No, but we stretch it out a while longer. Sooner or later, I'll be replaced as sheriff..."

I made a face. "What if they like you so much, they decide to keep you?"

He laughed. "I doubt that, but even so. Sooner or later, King Richard will return to England and put an end to the injustices Prince John has imposed. So we only need to keep this up until then."

The biggest *only* ever, but Daniel was right.

I let out a long breath, then spoke, trying to bolster my courage for lonely times to come. "So, you'll stay on as Nottingham's hottest sheriff..."

He rolled his eyes, but I went on.

"...meanwhile, I'll go on pining for you from Sherwood Forest, taking my frustrations out on any rich, arrogant bastard who happens to pass. Together, we'll make sure those who profit are those who need it most. And someday..." I let a weary beat pass, not fully convinced. "Someday, when a permanent sheriff is appointed — or when King Richard returns, Lord willing — we'll both declare our work done and retire."

Daniel nodded. "Exactly. Then we can start our happily-ever-after."

I let out a frustrated grumble. "And until then?"

Daniel nuzzled his jaw against mine, letting his stubble scrape my skin. "We'll keep meeting. Three Rivers Tavern... Up here... Maybe even in the monastery..."

I laughed out loud. "The monastery?"

"Well, you do seem to have an ally in that friar..."

I chuckled. Tuck might turn out to be helpful in ways I'd ever imagined.

Daniel went on, alternating kisses and ideas. "We could meet every full moon... Every Monday... You could even come to my place on market days..."

"Your place?" I laughed. "Robynne Hood, making booty calls to the sheriff of Nottingham?"

He shrugged. "They think Robin is a man."

I laughed. "That will just make the rumors juicier."

He laughed on his way to kissing my left breast. "I don't care what they say, think, or do. I only care about you."

With that, he licked the rosy tip of my nipple, sending heat waves through me. I wrapped my leg around his hip and nudged him closer. Closer...

Daniel was getting as breathless as I. Still, he had enough wherewithal to chuckle and pause.

"What?" I protested. Why stall at a time like this?

"Just thinking. Here we are, the sheriff and the outlaw..."

I snorted. "I make the rules in Sherwood Forest, and I say, quit talking and make love to me, you foolish dragon."

His lips played over my skin. "Yes, ma'am."

Daniel might have been the dragon, but within minutes, I was the one huffing and puffing. Stretching back languidly, opening my body to his for legendary lovemaking, as my uncouth brother might say.

Daniel grinned, reading my mind. When he spoke, his words were laced with love, passion, and desire. "Legendary is you, Robynne Hood. Now lie back and enjoy."

Enjoy I did, and enjoy I would, I decided. Now and in every future meeting we managed to pull off until the happy day when we could stay together... forever.

The stars winked as our bodies locked in a sensual dance. The moon shone as we lay together for hours afterward, too. When it grew cold, we both shifted into animal form, and Daniel lifted his wing to let me in.

I curled up under that snug shelter, smiling at that echo of the past. Daniel wound his long dragon tail and neck around me, keeping me safe. I fluffed my tail, making him giggle.

Of course, in dragon-speak, a giggle came out as more of a roar, and I shushed him.

Quiet, I murmured into his mind. *We don't want the sheriff to find us, you know.*

He laughed. *Something tells me he knows about us.* Then he curled his wing, nudging me closer to the hard plates of his chest. *Now, sleep tight, my mate. And sweet dreams.*

My reply was bittersweet. *I only have one dream these days.*

I didn't need to explain, because the images I saw filling Daniel's mind were the same as mine. Images of us sharing a blissfully ordinary life on the same side of the law in a peaceful and prosperous place.

I closed my eyes and indulged myself in those fantasies, praying they would give me the strength I needed to wait. The longer I fantasized, the more the images took on a new quality. The focus grew sharper and more detailed. My heart thumped a little harder, and a new feeling sprouted in my soul. Not just hope of attaining joy someday, but joy itself. It was as if I had somehow jumped to the future to live those moments before they actually occurred.

Moments like waking up cuddled with Daniel in a big, comfortable bed — one I didn't recognize, but which I knew was mine, at least in the future. I saw the two of us strolling casually across Nottingham's market square, our arms linked. We nodded our greetings to the people around us, which they returned just as pleasantly.

I saw the two of us in a lush field where an older, grayer version of Charger grazed, enjoying more peaceful days. Daniel stood beside him, balancing something on the steed's back. Something that took a while to come into focus. Not a saddle. Not a brush or a burden of some kind. What was it? I peered through time, trying to figure it out. And when I did...

My breath caught, and my heart thudded.

Daniel was right beside me — in real time, on that rock we lay upon, now face-to-face in human form. His eyes went wide at the same moment as mine, and his mouth opened a crack.

"Did you see that?" I whispered.

His throat bobbed, and he nodded, still in shock.

My heart pounded as I waited for him to confirm what he'd seen.

"I saw her," he whispered.

A joyful tear slipped from my eye, because I'd seen the same thing. "Our daughter."

"Riding Charger," Daniel filled in, his voice hoarse.

My lips curled. "More like, learning to ride Charger, with your help."

"She has your hair..." Daniel marveled, still in a whisper.

"...and your eyes," I finished. Blue as the summer sky and bright with joy and love. The love we showered on her, and the love we felt for each other. Love that had long since surmounted the barriers we faced today.

"It's the future," Daniel murmured in awe.

I leaned my forehead against his. "A good one."

More tears slipped from my eyes. Happy tears, because I knew that day would come. The path to that future was too murky to see, but the end point was brilliant with light. Our journey promised to be filled with challenges, but none of the kind we'd just endured. No more doubts about each other, no more uncertainty about how strong our love was. Only the outside world to overcome.

Daniel sighed, reading my mind. "Just that little detail, huh?"

I nodded — slowly at first, then more surely. "*Just*, because we'll tackle it together. Like you said, our own crusade."

He looked at me. "In the Crusades, we usually lined up and attacked — or defended — from a single, unified line."

I shrugged. "Well, we'll be using a new tactic — each of us working from a different side." I held my hands apart, then brought them gradually closer...closer...until my hands touched, palm to palm. "Until one day, there's no barrier any more. There will just be the two of us, together, ready to live that life we see."

Daniel's eyes shone in the darkness. "Just the two of us..." His smile grew. "Or should I say, just the three of us?"

My heart swelled at the thought of holding that blue-eyed girl in my arms someday. Or better yet, watching Daniel cuddle that blue-eyed girl in his strong arms.

"Maybe even the four of us, someday..." he mused. "Maybe even five..."

I laughed, putting a finger to his lips. "Let's not get ahead of ourselves."

His eyes sparkled — or were they simply reflecting mine? Either way, my soul lifted with joy and hope. Certainty, too. We might have a few more storms to weather, but the promised land was out there, and someday, we would step upon its shores. And what a moment that would be.

Daniel kissed my hand, echoing my thoughts. "What a moment that will be." Then he pulled me closer, and a moment later, he laughed.

I peeked at him quizzically.

He took a moment to marshal his thoughts, then went on. "My parents used to reminisce about the old days before I was born and when I was little. Even though those were tough times, they still smiled and focused on the good parts."

I thought of my dear dad, doing the same. For all the tears he'd shed over losing my mother, he'd flashed just as many loving smiles.

"Maybe that will be us someday. Reminiscing about the good old days," Daniel concluded. "Which means now."

I sighed, wishing the present gave us a little more *good* to celebrate. But Daniel shook his head.

"This *is* good. Look at us."

I chuckled, peering down at my chest, squeezed against his. "Yes, look at us."

"Any complaints, ma'am?" he asked in his best sheriff voice.

I chuckled. "No, sir."

The more I considered, the more I realized he was right. Someday, we would look back on these times and reminisce.

"So, from this moment on, we savor every minute we spend together," he declared. "We don't wish time to pass until we get to better days. We make the better days start now."

I nodded, vowing to do exactly that. To treasure every moment, no matter how big or how small. To live in the present and make the most of every stolen kiss, every secret encounter.

There was a mischievous element to it all that made my fox wag her tail.

I like the sound of that. Starting with every stolen kiss...

"Speaking of which," I murmured, tipping my chin up.

Daniel grinned at me. "No time like the present."

Whatever he tried to say next was muffled by my kiss. Then he gave up on words entirely and let his actions speak instead.

Actions that soon had both of us panting, sweating, moaning in ecstasy. . .

I danced my hands over my lover's back as he moved inside me. Just when I thought I would explode with pleasure, Daniel paused and let his eyes ask, *Dragon kiss?*

I grinned. Hell yes.

Then I winked and opened my mouth under his, anticipating the electrifying burst of fire.

No time like the present, my love.

∞∞∞∞

Dear reader — don't despair! Robynne and Daniel will soon get their happily-ever-after. I wish they could get it now, but the situation in Nottingham doesn't yet allow it. They will unite for good, though, once the events of Books 2 and 3 play out. Remember, good things come to those who wait!

I promise to make it all worthwhile, with John getting his love story in Book 2 and Tuck earning his in Book 3. That's the grand finale, in which Robynne and Daniel get their full happily-ever-after too. In the meantime, you'll get to see lots more of Robynne and Daniel, and you'll have fun unlocking the mysteries that John and Tuck harbor.

Where did the quiet bear shifter get his scars, for instance, and what do they have to do with his destined mate? How does Tuck escape his lonely life — and who is the lucky woman who helps him along the way? You'll find out in Books 2 and 3 of this series, and you'll get to see Robynne and Daniel together forever too. Happy reading!

Sneak Peek: Tempting the Outlaw

You just can't count on an outlaw these days...

I'm Willa Scarlet, and my mother taught me never to depend on a man. Case in point: my secret mission to keep a trunk full of priceless treasure safe from Prince John. When the outlaws of Sherwood Forest fail to help, all my carefully laid plans are thrown askew. And it's all the fault of one burly, infuriating bandit who has a bee in his bonnet when it comes to me. Men!

I'm John Little, bear shifter, and I can assure you, there's nothing little about me. I've also got a big dose of *stubborn* — and an issue with humans. I'm perfectly content with my reclusive life in the forest until Willa Scarlet saunters along. Now, I want the bite-sized redhead with an oversized attitude as far away as possible — the farther, the better.

The only things Willa and I have in common are sizzling chemistry, ruthless enemies, and responsibility for a treasure more valuable than either of us suspected. Before we know it, we're on the run, deep in trouble and in love, even if neither of us is ready to admit it. But we can't hide away forever, and soon, I'm forced to make hard choices. Do I follow my heart or my head? And where does my allegiance lie — with Willa, or with the shifters of Sherwood Forest?

Books by Anna Lowe

Sherwood Forest Shifters

Tempting the Sheriff (Book 1)

Tempting the Outlaw (Book 2)

Tempting the Maiden (Book 3)

Aloha Shifters - Jewels of the Heart

Lure of the Dragon (Book 1)

Lure of the Wolf (Book 2)

Lure of the Bear (Book 3)

Lure of the Tiger (Book 4)

Love of the Dragon (Book 5)

Lure of the Fox (Book 6)

Aloha Shifters - Pearls of Desire

Rebel Dragon (Book 1)

Rebel Bear (Book 2)

Rebel Lion (Book 3)

Rebel Wolf (Book 4)

Rebel Heart (A prequel to Book 5)

Rebel Alpha (Book 5)

Fire Maidens - Billionaires & Bodyguards

Fire Maidens: Paris (Book 1)

Fire Maidens: London (Book 2)

Fire Maidens: Rome (Book 3)

Fire Maidens: Portugal (Book 4)

Fire Maidens: Ireland (Book 5)

Fire Maidens: Scotland (Book 6)

Fire Maidens: Venice (Book 7)

Fire Maidens: Greece (Book 8)

Fire Maidens: Switzerland (Book 9)

The Wolves of Twin Moon Ranch

Desert Hunt (the Prequel)

Desert Moon (Book 1)

Desert Blood (Book 2)

Desert Fate (Book 3)

Desert Heart (Book 4)

Desert Rose (Book 5)

Desert Roots (Book 6)

Desert Destiny (Book 7)

Sasquatch Surprise (Book 8)

Desert Yule (a short story)

Desert Wolf: Complete Collection (Four short stories)

Blue Moon Saloon

Perfection (a short story prequel)

Damnation (Book 1)

Temptation (Book 2)

Redemption (Book 3)

Salvation (Book 4)

Deception (Book 5)

Celebration (a holiday treat)

Shifters in Vegas

Paranormal romance with a zany twist

Gambling on Trouble

Gambling on Her Dragon

Gambling on Her Bear

Gambling on Her Panther

Serendipity Adventure Romance

Off the Charts

Uncharted

Entangled

Windswept

Adrift

Travel Romance

Veiled Fantasies

Island Fantasies

www.annalowebooks.com

About the Author

USA Today and Amazon bestselling author Anna Lowe loves putting the "hero" back into heroine and letting location ignite a passionate romance. She likes a heroine who is independent, intelligent, and imperfect – a woman who is doing just fine on her own. But give the heroine a good man – not to mention a chance to overcome her own inhibitions – and she'll never turn down the chance for adventure, nor shy away from danger.

Anna loves dogs, sports, and travel – and letting those inspire her fiction. On any given weekend, you might find her hiking in the mountains or hunched over her laptop, working on her latest story. Either way, the day will end with a chunk of dark chocolate and a good read.

Visit AnnaLoweBooks.com

Printed in Great Britain
by Amazon

33103079R00108